Southern Comfort

Southern Comfort

Skyy

www.urbanbooks.net

Urban Books, LLC
97 N18th Street
Wyandanch, NY 11798

ISBN 13: 978-1-60162-684-4
ISBN 10: 1-60162-684-3

First Trade Paperback Printing March 2015
Printed in the United States of America

10 9 8 7 6 5 4 3 2 1

This is a work of fiction. Any references or similarities to actual events, real people, living or dead, or to real locales are intended to give the novel a sense of reality. Any similarity in other names, characters, places, and incidents is entirely coincidental.

Distributed by Kensington Publishing Corp.
Submit orders to:
Customer Service
400 Hahn Road
Westminster, MD 21157-4627
Phone: 1-800-733-3000
Fax: 1-800-659-2436

For my good friend Sadiece “Dice” Holland and our Epic European Adventure.

Acknowledgments

I AM SPARTACUS!

Yes, I literally jumped up and yelled that as I pressed save on my computer. This book was the most difficult writing experience of my whole career but I fucking did it!! This is my first full-length novel since *Full Circle* and the *Choices* series. I loved that writing experience so much that it made it very difficult to write this book. I completely questioned my writing ability. Was *Choices* just some amazing fluke? Could I write a full book without the comfort of my regular characters? I thought about having a cameo from Lena or Cooley, but decided it was best to leave the series alone and focus on writing something else. I still fear that people are going to hate this book, and honestly some people might, but I hope people love it as much as I loved writing it.

Sitting here listening to my beloved Bruno Mars, I am reflecting on this amazing year I had. Not only did I go out of the country for the first time, but I went to six amazing places in that one trip alone. Also I attended two comic book conventions, and attended another amazing Bruno Mars concert. This honestly was the best year of my life and I still have four more months left in the year. I still wake up sometimes wishing I was still standing at the Coliseum or walking down an alley in Venice.

There are three people I want to mention in this dedication and those are the three people who got me out of my comfort zone this year.

First and the big one is Sadiece. There were so many times that I sat around wanting to go to new places and even times that trips were planned but fell through with other people. Yet while sitting on Facebook messenger I told you I wanted to go to Europe and you said "sure, why not." From there we planned the Epic European Adventure. Most people thought I was never going to go through with it, but we did. Thank you for showing me your world and letting me see that everything doesn't have to go according to plan, and that I have to go with the flow sometimes. From coffee shops and French fries in Amsterdam to watching me live one of my dreams of yelling "I am Spartacus" in the Coliseum, I can't thank you enough for actually going on the trip with me. I can't wait to see more places and get more stamps in my passport now. You bloody rock! (Yes, I had to say bloody at least one time.)

The other two people I need to mention are Maya and Aaliyah. You guys have no idea how happy I am to have met you. Besides our love for Spartacus, with you guys I have been able to feel comfortable in my own skin and do things that even I felt I would never do. I can't wait for us to have more adventures together.

Lastly I want to thank my fans who I cherish so much. I continue to do this because you guys keep me motivated. I stalled for so long on this book simply because I didn't want to let you guys down and I know this book is going to be different but I hope you all like it.

So to everyone, stop being afraid to try new things and don't let fear keep you from going places you've always wanted to go. Take some time, plan the trip, give yourself enough time to pay for it, and GO. Trust me, you won't regret it.

Chapter 1

Willow ran her hand against the wall until finally finding the light switch. She turned on the lights and stood in her empty flat. Everything looked the same outside of the table covered with fashion and design magazines. She was rather surprised to find it tidy besides the layers of dust on her ceiling fan and furniture pieces Piper probably never used. She knew she could trust her friend Piper to pick up her mail and watch her television, but cleaning was out of her friendship pay grade.

Willow put her suitcase on the floor and walked to her bedroom. The bed was unmade, probably due to Piper using her place after a long night of partying. Her closet door was open. She knew Piper probably had a few of her dresses in her possession. She would have to do inventory on another day.

Willow fell back on her bed. She wondered if Piper slept with anyone in her bed. As much as the idea grossed her out, it wasn't enough to make her get up. She was exhausted and only wanted to rest. She pulled her large comforter over her head, blocking the sunlight coming in through her window.

It was quiet; the darkness had a calming effect over her. Her last day at home played vividly in her mind. She could hear her father's voice crystal clear alerting her that his cancer was back and more aggressive. Nothing else mattered. She threw a few clothes in a bag and left and she hadn't been back for almost a year. Willow stayed with her father at the family estate until he took his final breath.

A looming feeling of uncertainty filled her. What was next for her? She no longer had school or family obligations. After making her father happy and completing university she followed her dream and completed London College of Fashion. Just as she was ready to attack the fashion world she got the call from her father. For the first time in her life she was completely free to do whatever she wanted to do.

Could she just pick up where she left off? She thought about interning with a fashion designer, or possibly opening her own little store selling her original designs. The thought of fashion seemed trivial while her father was sick, and even thinking of it now didn't light the fire inside she expected it to. The thought of any kind of work only made her feel more exhausted.

Traveling entered her mind. With the money her father left her she was able to do anything she wanted. The idea of going anywhere she wanted to go did sound exciting. She was already well traveled. She had been to practically every major country in Europe. Maybe it was time to tackle another region, Asia, or even America.

An emptiness settled in the pit of her stomach. Who would she travel with? She knew Piper would be down but they had different ideas of travel. Where Willow wanted to really dive into the culture and history of a place, Piper only wanted to experience the nightlife. She remembered their trip to Amsterdam: while she explored the amazing museums, Piper slept off the hangover from the night before.

Willow pulled her cell phone out of her pocket. She scrolled to a name on her contact list. She stared at the picture of Lisa, the last woman she had dated before her father got sick. Lisa was a sexy, aggressive DJ she met out one night with Piper, and they spent many steamy nights together. But Willow knew it wouldn't be anything more. Lisa might have been hot but she lacked any depth to her. Willow couldn't hold a single real conversation with Lisa outside of what was going on in the gay world of London.

Willow sighed. The one thing she knew for sure was that she wanted to finally meet someone special. Willow spent countless nights holding on to a teddy bear and crying herself to sleep while her father was sick. It made her long for something real, something that she watched in movies and read in books. Willow wondered, were soul mates real? Could she have a deeper connection with someone outside of just the physical? It had to exist, and she wanted to find . . . It.

Willow knew there was only one person to call. She picked up her phone, scrolling to her only real friend's phone number.

"Willz, darling, how the hell are ya?" a bubbly voice echoed through the phone.

Willow pressed the speaker button on her phone. "Hey, Piper, I'm back."

Willow couldn't help but shake her head as her friend let out a high pitched squeal.

"I am headed to Johnny's house for a house party. I'm totally on my way to pick you up. It's time for you to have some fun again."

Before Willow could protest Piper hung the phone up. Willow sighed. She didn't want to go but the idea of spending the night in her dusty flat didn't sound fun either. She got up, pulled her curly hair back into a ponytail, and headed to her shower.

The party was filled with the same faces Willow always saw. She greeted people and answered the same questions she was asked all night like where had she been and was she still single. Two girls who had already tried to talk to her at previous parties attempted to try their luck again. Willow smiled, turning them down just as easily as she did the first time.

Piper was in rare form as usual. Like most of the people from their boarding school, Piper was rich and finished school only to become a socialite. Her long, blond hair hung down her back almost reaching the overpriced jeans that were so tight everyone knew she couldn't have on underwear with them.

"Willz, dance with me," Piper slurred as she wrapped her long arms around Willow.

Willow swayed to the music with her friend who was obviously very drunk. Piper hung on to her in an attempt to stay on both feet. Willow quickly noticed a few people watching them, in hopes that the dance would turn into a heavy make-out session, something that usually happened when Piper danced with women.

"Pipe, I think I'm going to head home," Willow shouted over the loud music.

"Why? We just bloody got here," Piper protested.

"We have been here three hours, hon."

Piper took a step back. The confused look on her face let Willow know that she had obviously lost track of time as usual.

"Okay, let me get my coat and we can head out," Piper said before disappearing in the crowd.

Willow walked over to the door. Three minutes passed and there was no sign of Piper. Willow made her way through the crowded dance floor only to find Piper talking to her ex-girlfriend Corrie. Willow sighed. She was very familiar with the back and forth dance that Corrie and Piper continued to dance.

"Hey, Pipe, I'm gonna grab a cab and get out of here," Willow said as she walked up to the two women.

"See, you idiot, you made me forget I was leaving with Willow," Piper yelled at her ex.

"Hey, Corrie," Willow said to the spiky-haired butch girl.

Corrie nodded her head while holding on to Piper. "Hey, Willow, it's been a long time. Don't worry, I'll make sure she gets home safe," Corrie said in her soft voice.

Willow nodded her head and turned around, hearing Piper yelling at Corrie the whole time. Willow grabbed the first black cab she saw. She stared at the lights of her city passing landmarks that visitors gawked at on a daily basis. Soon they were on her quiet street. She paid the cab driver and headed to her flat.

Even though the idea of a tumultuous relationship like Piper and Corrie's had made her want to cringe, she couldn't help but admire the fact that they would end up spending the night together. As Willow crawled into her favorite side of her bed, she wondered when someone would occupy the other half.

"So are you going to say anything?"

It felt like high noon in the loft that Katrina and Saura shared together. Saura ran her fingers through her wavy black hair. She stood on the opposite side of the room watching her girlfriend, who was sitting in a chair looking at the floor. This moment had played through Saura's head a million times in the last three weeks. She expected a much different reaction. She expected her hard but gentle girlfriend to try to get her to stay. She expected anger, tears, resentment, but never silence.

"Tree, please say something," Saura begged, unsure of how to handle the silence between them.

Katrina stared at her right foot. She had never been so happy to have on one of her many pairs of Jordans;

the thick shoe hid the fact that her feet wouldn't stop trembling. She never knew why, but whenever she was upset her feet would be the first thing to start trembling.

"When are you leaving?"

Katrina asked the question but wouldn't raise her head. She couldn't look at her beautiful girlfriend in that moment. She knew that looking at her would break her and that was the one thing she didn't want. In the back of her mind she always knew Memphis was a rest stop for Saura; she was stunningly beautiful. Katrina always joked with Saura that her African American mother and Asian father broke the mold when they created her, which was why she didn't have any siblings. Saura's Asian bloodline showed in her long, wavy hair that came down to the middle of her butt, and her tight brown eyes. However, she got her body from her mother. Saura was tall with a curvy body with hips and ass that Katrina couldn't get enough of.

"Three days," Saura responded.

Katrina took a deep breath. It was now very obvious that she was upset; even her shoe couldn't hide the shaking. She knew the day was coming. Saura had been dabbling in modeling locally for a long time. All the best photographers in the city had shot her and called her whenever they had a special project they wanted to shoot just for their personal portfolios. She was making a name for herself, now working as a spokesmodel for the local promotional teams for liquor companies and Coors beer. She had mentioned expanding but it was always just a passing thought. Katrina never saw her actually trying to do anything. All of a sudden she had an agent who was flying her out to Los Angeles and putting her up in a model house with a bunch of other models.

"Saura, damn! I need a better explanation. I didn't even know you were looking for an agent."

"I didn't want to say anything because I didn't know if anything was ever going to come of it. But when they contacted me I knew that I needed to look into this."

"And when exactly did they contact you?" Katrina finally looked up at her girlfriend who was nervously fidgeting with a piece of her hair.

"A few weeks ago," Saura mumbled under her breath.

Katrina's eyes felt like they were going to pop out of her head. "Wait what did you just say?" Katrina shook her head in disbelief.

"I got the offer about a month ago." Saura threw her head down. Now she couldn't look at Katrina.

Without even knowing Katrina jumped out of the chair. "You are fucking kidding me. So you knew you were going to do this shit a month ago and you waited 'til three days before you leave to fucking tell me?" Katrina's whole body was trembling.

Saura finally raised her head and looked at Katrina. "I was scared; I didn't know how to tell you."

"How about the same way you are telling me now!" Katrina threw her hands up. "Fuck, Saura, how could you fucking do this?"

"I was scared. I didn't want to hurt you and I also didn't want you trying to change my mind."

Katrina's whole body froze. She fell back down in the chair putting her hands on her mouth. Recent memories started flashing in her mind. Things were starting to make sense. Saura was suddenly constantly taking clothes to Goodwill claiming she didn't want them anymore. She had already gotten rid of most of her winter clothes, Katrina knew now she wouldn't need sweaters and coats in L.A.

"Tree, I love you so much and I knew that if I told you either you would try to get me to stay or you would try to follow me. You have your trip to Europe coming up and your restaurant. I couldn't let you stop all of that just for me."

"Our trip,"

"What?"

"It was supposed to be our trip to Europe. Remember that, Saura? It was the trip we planned together."

"I know, Tree, but this is my dream, just like Europe and the restaurant is your dream. I can't let you not go, just like I can't say no to this."

Katrina was at a loss for words. She knew that Saura was right. She always wanted to be a chef and one day open a restaurant. She graduated top of her culinary class and was finally taking the trip to Europe she always wanted to take. Their plan to spend the month hitting different countries and trying different foods and wines was something Katrina had been waiting for. They were supposed to leave in a week; now she didn't want to go at all.

"You could have told me. We could have had time to work this out. We are in a relationship, Saura, we can make this work."

Katrina noticed the tears falling down Saura's face. She opened her arms as Saura walked up to her. Saura sat in her lap and Katrina wrapped her arms around her. Katrina wanted to break down but she wasn't going to allow herself to. She didn't want Saura knowing the truth. She was worried.

"Don't cry, babe, this can be a good thing for both of us. We are getting all the things that we dreamed about. One day we will be the power couple. The hot chef and the supermodel." Katrina smiled.

Saura turned her face to Katrina. She pressed her lips against Katrina's.

Katrina never imagined falling in love. She always saw herself as the lone wolf who only had temporary affairs.

Things changed the moment Saura walked into the club. She had to have her, and so did every other stud in the building. However, Katrina was the one who won the prize in the end, and they had been together for two years strong.

Saura stood up in front of Katrina. She didn't want to think about either one of their upcoming trips. She pulled the string holding her halter dress around her neck. The dress slid down her body until falling to the floor. Her matching blue bra and panties set looked like it was painted on her.

Katrina kissed Saura's flat stomach. She put her hands on each side of Saura's side. Katrina sat on the edge of the chair as she pulled Saura's panties down. She didn't want to waste any time; after all they didn't have much time left together. Katrina stood up. Katrina unsnapped Saura's bra as they walked to their king-sized bed.

Saura crawled to the top of their bed allowing Katrina to admire her ass as she moved. Katrina didn't give her time to turn over. She jumped on the bed grabbing Saura from behind. Her tongue fiercely entered Saura from behind as Saura held on to the headboard.

Katrina didn't want to be soft; she sucked Saura's clit while her index and middle finger found her G-spot instantly. Katrina's fingers aggressively attacked Saura's spot causing a rush of her sweetness to cover her fingers and trickle out of her. Katrina licked all of her woman's sweetness sucking Saura's lady lips before focusing back on her swollen clit.

Saura let out moans of pleasure as her body tensed from the hurting Katrina was putting on her. She knew one thing: Katrina knew her body better than she did. Katrina knew every spot to hit to send her body into an erotic frenzy. Katrina was the first to not only make love to her body, but to her spirit.

Katrina wanted to please Saura more than ever. Maybe if she made her remember all that she had here she wouldn't leave. She knew it was incredibly selfish but she didn't care. Saura's body began to shake. She hit the headboard over and over in an attempt to tap out from the hurting Katrina was putting on her. Erotic whimpers of pure pleasure echoed through the room. Saura's body didn't belong to her anymore; it was Katrina's and Katrina knew it. Katrina refused to stop; she wanted Saura to remember this moment and every moment they had ever had together. Saura was the first woman Katrina had ever truly given her heart and Katrina wasn't going to let go easily. Katrina knew in her mind she couldn't lose her girl, and she had three days to convince her that Saura belonged in Memphis with her.

Saura couldn't take any more. Her body went limp, falling down on their comfortable memory foam mattress. She balled up in her spot as Katrina wrapped her arm around her, slowly rubbing the goose bumps that covered Saura's arm. Katrina kissed the nape of Saura's neck.

"We can make this work, Saura. If any couple could make this work I know it's us," Katrina whispered.

Saura didn't respond; she put her hand on Katrina's hand. For the first time since finding out the news Saura actually believed there was a possibility it could work. They both fell asleep with thoughts of the future on their minds.

Teri watched as Porsha sang along to a song on the radio. Teri couldn't wait to drop her off as her attempts to hit the high notes were about to work her last nerve. She knew the end was near for Porsha. Teri met her two months ago at a gas station; she spotted the short, thick girl as she was walking toward the store from the bus stop. Shaped like an hourglass with super thick thighs and a flat stomach, Teri knew she was going to try to pull her the moment she noticed the rainbow keychain hanging from her plastic purse.

Teri walked into the store to see the girl mixing a bunch of different slush flavors together in a giant Styrofoam cup. Teri was glad she had her short, spiked haircut lined the day before, as it was lying perfectly to her head. She waited until she saw Porsha walking to the line. Teri jumped in line, grabbing a bag of candy.

"Ring mine up and whatever she is having," Teri said as she handed her American Express to the cashier. Teri walked out without looking back. She pushed the keyless entry to her Mercedes and waited for a moment.

"Excuse me," a voice called out.

Teri placed her shades on her head and turned around.

"You told the lady in there to pay for my stuff?" Porsha questioned.

"Yeah, enjoy." Teri opened her car door.

Porsha rushed up to the door, grabbing it before she closed it. "But why you do that?" Porsha dropped her head to the side.

"Because I like treating beautiful women when I see them."

Just like that Porsha was putty in Teri's hands. She spent the next two months sexing Porsha at her every whim. She didn't have to spend money; Porsha was just happy to spend time in Teri's beautiful house. She always seemed astonished when Teri showed her anything new. Teri introduced her to Olive Garden, Bahamas Breeze, and local Memphis spots. By the time Teri took her to Rafferty's, Porsha was ready to marry her.

Teri pulled into the daycare center that Porsha worked at. Porsha turned her body toward Teri, flashing a huge smile as she tossed all twenty-eight inches of store-bought hair to the side. Teri tried to focus on her face, even though she loved looking at the double Ds Porsha had. Even though she knew she was going to be ending it, she was going to hate giving up those breasts.

"Last night was amazing, as usual." Porsha smiled as she leaned in kissing Teri on her cheek.

"It was," Teri said as she rubbed her fingers against Porsha's nipple that was protruding through her thin, tight shirt.

Porsha purred; she shifted her body in the leather seat. "You better stop 'for I'm late to work." Porsha pushed her body closer allowing Teri to get a better feel.

"You better stop before you don't make it to work at all."

Teri grabbed the back of Porsha's head, planting her lips against Porsha's thick, pouty lips. Teri knew that was another thing she was going to miss; Porsha's lips were thick, soft, and she truly knew how to use them.

Porsha hopped out of the car. She pulled her tight jeans up. They left a gap showing off the curve in her back, which only made her butt look even better. Teri instantly started rethinking her decision to cut her loose, but she knew it would only be a matter of time before cute would become clingy and possessive.

Besides sex Teri knew she had nothing in common with Porsha, which was the way she liked her women. Even though she didn't come from wealth like her best friends, Teri worked hard to gain the position that she had as a pharmacist. Although a sweet girl, Porsha lacked depth and intelligence. She couldn't hold a conversation outside of Stevie J and Joseline and frowned whenever Teri tried to watch anything remotely educational.

Teri's friends constantly mocked her choices in women. They didn't understand why she would waste time on women she knew she could never have anything real with.

Teri knew exactly what she was doing. She didn't want something serious; she preferred her women sexy but stupid. Nothing made her happier than to date a chick who viewed her as their come up. They would put her on a pedestal for the smallest things. A meal at Red Lobster was a luxury. If she dated someone like one of her friends they would curse her out just for considering Red Lobster as a suitable place for fine dining.

Porsha was a little different than most. Where most of the girls looked at Teri as their come up, a way to get cheddar biscuits and real designer bags, Porsha just wanted to hang out. Being a daughter of a mother who had seven kids, she was very frugal and excellent at playing house. She often made comments about the prices of places they went to eat, saying that money could be saved and she could just cook.

After one of their sex sessions, she would get up, cook an amazing late-night snack, and make sure Teri's house was spotless. As much as Teri loved that part, she knew in the end she needed someone with more to offer. Porsha would cater to Teri, but couldn't do anything to advance herself. Teri often tried to talk to her about enrolling in community college or some night classes. Porsha would say she would think about it, but never did anything.

Teri knew the time was coming to an end when Porsha asked her where were they going "home" one night after a movie. Whenever a girl started to consider her house as home it was time to get rid of them. She knew it was better to end it than continue to make the girl think she actually had a chance. Teri shook her head; it was going to suck but it had to be done. It was time to find a new body for the other side of her bed.

Chapter 2

"That's fucked up, dude. Three days, she is wrong as fuck for that," Teri huffed while she peddled on her bike.

Katrina joined her two best friends for their bike ride down the Memphis Green line, a new bike path and walking trail that ran through half of the city. Katrina expected that reaction from her loudmouth friend. She looked over at her other friend, Devon, who had on professional bike gear from head to toe. Her ponytail had turned from straight to kinky from the humidity and her sweat.

"Come on, Teri, you have to see where she is coming from. Katrina isn't the easiest person to talk to," Devon replied as they passed two women power walking on the side.

"What do you mean I'm not easy to talk to?"

"You know you aren't. If she would have told you this a month ago you would have tried everything in your might to get her to stay." Devon held her hand up to let another biker know to pass her.

"Or she would have just broken up with her to avoid the pain," Teri added.

"Whoa, whoa what the hell are you guys trying to say?" Katrina hit the brakes on her bike. The other two friends stopped the moment they realized Katrina was no longer moving. "I resent those statements, bitches." Katrina folded her arms.

Her two friends looked at each other confused.

"We are not talking about some random chick from the past; we are talking about Saura. You know how much I love that girl. When have I ever felt this way about anyone?"

"Well there was Brandy, and Kim." Teri counted on her fingers.

"And don't forget LaMonique," Devon joked.

Katrina threw both of her middle fingers up at her friends. Two guys sped by on their bikes as if they were in a race.

"I liked them but you guys know that Saura was different. Hell we've been together for two, almost three years." Katrina sighed.

"Okay, yes, it's true, Saura is the first real relationship you have had. I can understand why you are upset but knowing you I can understand why she did it. She was probably terrified of hurting you," Devon said as she jogged in place.

"I still think it shows a true lack of compassion to wait 'til three days before you are leaving to tell the woman you have been with for two years that you are leaving. Who the hell does that? I mean you guys have a place together, bills and shit," Teri said as she retied the black silk scarf she had holding her freshly done hair in place. She was the epitome of a soft stud; you would never catch her in a dress, but her short haircut would always be laid to perfection.

"Well the house is in my name. I pay the bills," Katrina replied.

"Yeah, but, Katrina, she talked you into buying the house. You were fine in your condo," Devon pointed out causing Katrina to shoot her the evil eye. "I'm just saying." Devon shrugged her shoulders.

"Well I'm just saying that shit was shady as hell." Teri patted Katrina on her back.

"She was scared," Devon added. "People do things when they are scared that they normally wouldn't do."

Teri rolled her eyes. "Still, it says something about the person. It shows a total lack of regard for you and your feelings. You don't have time to plan anything. Not to mention she knew how badly you were looking forward to the trip to Europe. Now you are supposed to go by yourself?"

Teri continued to rant while Katrina thought about her statement. With all that was happening she hadn't thought about the fact that now she would be in a foreign country by herself. It was her first trip out of the country.

"She will be fine, Teri. It's just Europe," Devon chimed in noticing the worried expression on Katrina's face.

"Whatever, bro. Didn't you watch *Taken?*"

Katrina knew her friends were like night and day. She had known Devon since grade school. They went to the same private school for most of their life. Katrina and Devon both came from successful parents, but Devon was a completely trust fund baby. Katrina's mother was living off the money left to her by Katrina's father who was a pro football player for years. Her father passed away years ago leaving a small nest egg for them, but nowhere near the money that Devon came from.

Katrina met Teri while attending college at Rhodes University. Teri put on a hard front, but she was the smartest person Katrina had ever met. She had a full ride to Rhodes and went on to become a pharmacist. Although incredibly intelligent, the world she grew up in was completely different from that of Devon and Katrina. The first time she had ever been on an airplane was when they took an *Olivia* all-lesbian vacation to Mexico.

"Katrina, ignore her, you aren't backpacking across Europe. Hell you aren't even staying in a hotel that's less than four stars. All you need to do is book you a couple of tours and use the hop-on, hop-off busses and you will be just fine."

"Still, what about her expensive-ass ticket you paid for, and the train tickets and transfers?" Teri protested.

"She said she would pay me back for that," Katrina mumbled.

"How? She doesn't have a real job." Teri threw her hands up.

"Maybe she'll book a big movie." Devon smiled.

"Yeah, okay." The deadpan expression on Teri's face made Devon laugh.

Katrina thought about her trip. She wasn't a stranger to traveling but there was a big difference in being in a foreign country and not on a cruise ship or resort. Now she was supposed to navigate Europe all alone? "Maybe I should postpone the trip until you can come with me, Dev."

"Why?" Devon's head snapped around to Katrina. "Tree, don't do that. You have been waiting your whole life to do something like this. Think of all the amazing food you are going to try. If not for anything else, you need this for your restaurant."

"Now don't get me wrong, I don't like the idea of you going alone, but I really don't like the idea of you giving up your dreams because Saura is living hers."

The three friends looked at each other. Katrina knew they were right. Ever since she found her love of culinary arts she wanted to travel to Europe. Katrina shook her head and started riding her bike again.

"Look I haven't decided what to do about Europe yet. I have a few weeks to think about that, however, I have two days to figure out what to do about Saura. Do we try this long distance thing? Or maybe I should consider moving to the West Coast."

Both friends quickly began to protest the idea of Katrina leaving Memphis.

"It would be incredibly selfish of me to try to get her to stay; she would never have the opportunities to act and model if she stays in Memphis," Katrina said while she looked straight ahead.

"It would be incredibly stupid to try to move all the way across the country for a chick." Teri rolled her eyes.

"Tree, you are opening a restaurant. You have been working on this for over a year. Think of all the money you have put into it. You can't just up and leave that either," Devon said as she rode past Katrina.

"Right! And especially not for a chick," Teri huffed.

"She's not just some chick." Katrina hated when her friend dismissed her relationship.

"Tree, you act like y'all been together for ten years and got kids and shit. You said yourself you don't even share bills."

"You are going to be working on it while I'm in Europe, why not run it full time?"

"'Cause it's your baby, not mine. I am just helping you out."

Katrina and Teri caught up to Devon.

"Fuck that, you aren't moving to another coast. Memphis is home," Teri interjected.

"Maybe be bicoastal." Devon glanced at Katrina.

"Shit, there isn't anything bi about this girl." Teri's joke made them all laugh.

The three made it back to their cars. They packed their bikes on their bike racks.

"All I know is that I love her. I don't want to lose her over something like this. I never thought I would find someone I cared about this much. I can't lose her now. And if that means making some sacrifices then I guess I'm going to have to do that."

The friends said their good-byes and Katrina headed toward her apartment. She stopped at Saura's favorite florist and picked up a dozen peach roses, which were her favorite. Time wasn't on her side, and the battle between being selfish and selfless was driving her crazy. Could she make a long distance relationship work? The idea of sex via Skype didn't appeal to her. She wanted to feel Saura and taste her whenever she wanted to. She loved the idea of waking up to find her beauty lying next to her.

Katrina noticed Saura's car wasn't in the driveway. Her mind began to race. She wondered how long she would be gone. She could try to set up something special for Saura, maybe order some food from their favorite sushi restaurant. Katrina started thinking of making a nice surprise to show Saura how much she respected and loved her: flowers, candles, sushi, and amazing sex to end the night right.

Katrina walked in the house. For some reason something felt different. She turned the living room light on. An uneasy feeling came over her. Things just didn't seem right. She walked through the house and to the back room.

Katrina froze, dropping the dozen of flowers on the floor next to her.

The closet was open, and Saura's things were completely gone. She looked over at the dresser drawer that used to hold Saura's intimates; it was completely empty too. Sitting on the middle of the bed was a card with her name scribbled in Saura's handwriting. Katrina's heart was racing. She felt like she couldn't breathe. She sat on the edge of the bed and grabbed the card.

Katrina,

I know when you walk in the room you are going to be very upset with me. I know that I deserve it. I couldn't stay and I don't expect you to truly understand why. I know that you are thinking that we can make it work long distance. You might even be considering leaving Memphis. I can't let you do this. I can't allow you to put your dreams on hold, and I honestly don't want anything holding me back from the dreams I have. I love you, and I love you enough to completely let you go. I need to do this, and I need to do it alone. Please don't hate me.

Saura

Katrina read the final line again. As she reread the letter over and over, rage filled her body. She ripped the letter up and threw it on the ground. She picked her phone up and dialed Saura's number only to get a disconnected message. Saura not only left, but she changed her number. Katrina pressed the Facebook app on her phone. She tried to find Saura's name but it wasn't online. She searched only to find her profile was no longer there. She sent her an e-mail.

How could you do this to me, to us!

Katrina threw her phone and it shattered against the wall. She felt the room spinning. Katrina fell to her knees. She tried to stop it, but she couldn't control the emotions that were taking over her. She broke as tears began to roll. She cried, holding herself and rocking back and forth. Without any notice Saura had made the decision for them, and it was the one decision Katrina was not willing to consider. She was gone, and Katrina knew there was nothing she could do about it.

Willow woke up to find Piper lying on her sofa. She forgot that Piper had a key to her apartment. She decided to get back into her routine by going for her morning run. The ground was moist, obviously from an early morning rain. She jogged to the park stopping for a brief moment to stretch and catch her breath. The park in the morning was one of her favorite places. Nannies sat on benches while watching the children playing on the play set. Other men and women jogged around the path of the small neighborhood park.

Willow didn't know what was next for her besides cleaning her apartment. She knew finding the one was going to be harder than expected, especially being surrounded by the same lesbians she'd seen a million times already. Willow loved Piper but she knew she had to expand her social circle. Maybe she should start attending some of the higher society events that her father always urged her to attend. Willow just didn't see herself in that world, even though she grew up in it.

A woman in a beautiful flowing dress caught her attention. Willow admired the print on the skirt. Three designs flashed in her mind that she could create using the same pink floral print. The artist in her was now trying to break through the barriers of uncertainty that she had built up. As she studied the cut and design of the dress the itch to design was settling in her.

Willow couldn't deny the fact that she loved fashion and not at least trying to pursue her dream of a career in fashion sounded like a bad idea. The only thing that could stop her from opening her store was her own fears. She knew Piper loved stealing her original creations for her own personal wardrobe, but did that mean other people would want to wear her clothes?

Willow stopped at Starbucks and grabbed two lattes before heading back to her home. She opened the door and found Piper still knocked out. Willow sat on her coffee table and held one of the cups up next to Piper's face. It only took a second for Piper to smell the amazing aroma and wake up.

"Hello, honey," Piper said taking the cup from Willow.

"I just want to thank you for the smashing job you did dusting around this place." Willow ran her finger over the lamp sitting on the coffee table next to the couch. She held the dirty finger up.

"I got all your mail at least." Piper flashed her pearly whites.

Willow joined Piper on her couch. "So you didn't go home with Corrie I see." Willow sipped her latte.

Piper rolled her eyes. "I am so over her. Do you know she actually has a girlfriend now but was still trying to go home with me? Fucking hell if I did. I am so over her and her bullshit. Moving on, how are you, babes? How does it feel to be back in the big city?"

Willow shrugged her shoulders.

"Well there is a big party tonight at Heaven. Word on the street is that Gaga is going to do a surprise show, or maybe it was Madonna? Who cares, it going to be huge."

Willow stood up. "Yeah, the idea of spending the night dancing with a bunch of gay men doesn't sound appealing to me."

"There will be tons of girls there, too, you know. Time to get you back out in the dating world." Piper flung one of her long legs in the air. "Get someone in between those legs."

"Can you put that down?" Willow said as she pushed Piper's leg down.

"Seriously, girl, you have had some hard times. I want to see you have some fun."

Willow sat back down on the couch. "Hey, Pipe, have you ever been to America?"

Piper frowned. "Once with my family; we went to New York. I don't know why people get so excited over that place. It felt like here except with bad accents and ugly cabs. Why do you ask?"

"I feel like I'm torn. On one hand I really want to get into designing again," Willow said watching Piper's eyes brighten at the thought of new clothes for her to wear. "But on the other hand I want to experience something new. Hey how about we do it like we used to and hit a place for the weekend? Let's go to Paris or something."

Piper ran her hand through her long hair. "As great as that sounds I have a small problem. I have a job to go to."

"What?" Willow was shocked.

"My fucking parents are on this whole grownup kick and threatened to cut me off if I didn't start working at my father's stupid office. I spend my days in ugly heels fetching coffee like a bloody servant."

Willow couldn't believe her ears. She listened to Piper talk about working at her father's doctor's office. Her father was one of the best plastic surgeons in London who only did work for high-paying clients. Piper complained about the work, but couldn't help but love the idea of seeing all the famous people who came in for consultations or to get work done. Willow realized quickly that if Piper had a job it really meant it was time for her to figure her life out.

The two finished catching up before Piper had to leave to go get ready for work. Willow promised to think about going to Heaven. The club was the biggest gay club in London, and she hadn't been since way before her father got sick.

Willow closed the door behind her friend. She pulled out the only cleaning products she had in the house. She turned on a music station on her television and started cleaning. Two hours later her home was dust and dirt free and she was exhausted.

Willow opened her MacBook to check her e-mail. She didn't realize how long it had been since she checked e-mails. She had messages from old fashion school classmates and even one from a professor. She responded to all the messages and began looking at photos from Paris fashion week. On the side of one of the Web sites she was browsing she noticed an ad for a travel company. She clicked on the ad to see various exotic locations listed. There were so many places she could go.

The woman from the park crossed her mind. Willow opened her design software on her computer. She began to sketch a skirt on a woman's figure that came on the program. In moments she had redesigned the dress the woman was wearing, giving it a romantic but edgy feel.

Willow walked into her office. Rolls of fabric sat on the side next to two body forms with fabric pinned to them. Her sewing machine still had the orange thread that was in it from the last dress she created. She remembered that Piper quickly took the dress to wear to a party and got tons of compliments on it.

Willow studied a few of the sketches she had posted on her project board. She admired the fact that the things she created almost a year ago were still fashionable today. She picked out a sketch of a purple dress and decided that would be her first creation. There would be time for travel, but now it was time to work.

Chapter 3

"I knew that bitch wasn't shit," Teri said as she closed the door on Devon's Lexus.

"Can you not do that now? We have to be there for our friend. No bashing," Devon argued as she pushed her keyless entry.

The friends walked up the driveway of Katrina's house. She had bought her grandmother's house, which was in Whitehaven, one of the many neighborhoods of Memphis. Devon joked about Katrina living in the hood, but the truth was the part of neighborhood that Katrina lived in still was home to many well-off families. However, if you went down a few streets you would be surrounded by hair supply stores and chicken wing restaurants.

They could hear music coming from inside the house. Teri rang the doorbell again but got no answer. Devon called Katrina's phone, which instantly went to voicemail.

"I know she's in there; her car is in the garage," Devon declared, pointing at the open garage. "Maybe we should just come back."

"Fuck that," Teri hissed as she pulled her keys out of her pocket, fidgeting through the gold and silver keys on the ring until finding Katrina's spare key.

Teri opened the door and the two walked in.

"Tree," Devon yelled out. "Can you come out here?"

Both stood in the doorway not wanting to intrude too much.

“Bitch, either come out or we are coming in,” Teri yelled while dropping her keys on the coffee table. The two women walked to the back of the dark house.

Katrina’s door was cracked. The music grew louder and louder as the two walked closer to the bedroom. Teri pushed the door open to find Katrina lying on her back in her bed. She turned the light on while Devon turned down the music.

“You know when a person doesn’t answer that usually means they are busy or they don’t want to be bothered."Katrina mumbled without looking away from the ceiling.

“Yeah, well that’s when you don’t have friends to come and check on you.” Teri plopped down on the edge of the bed. Katrina still didn’t move.

“Saura called me,” Devon mumbled. “Are you okay?”

Katrina sat up. “So she called you? Funny that she can call you but didn’t have the common courtesy to call her girlfriend. Or should I say ex-girlfriend. Do you have her new number?”

Devon shook her head. “She called from a blocked number. I didn’t even speak to her. She left a voicemail telling me that she had made it to Los Angeles and what happened. Tree. I’m so sorry.”

Katrina got out of the bed. She started pacing the floor. “Don’t be sorry, I’m not. Obviously she did what she felt she needed to do. Fuck me and my feelings. Fuck the fact that I was going to be fucking hurting over this shit. Fuck it! Fuck her ’cause she completely fucked me!”

Katrina threw her hand over her dresser knocking all her bottles and belongings on the floor. The action caused Devon and Teri to jump.

“Whoa, dude, chill out. Yeah, what she did was fucked up but there’s no reason to fuck up your stuff because of what she did.” Teri jumped up and started picking the expensive bottles of cologne and things off of the floor.

Katrina fell back on her bed. Her head was spinning again. She buried her face into her hands. She didn't want her friends to see her cry, but she couldn't help it. "I fucking loved her. I gave her my all. I didn't deserve this shit!"

Devon sat next to Katrina. She put her arm around her hurting friend. "Katrina, I know it's hard to understand but I think that Saura did what she thought was going to be best. You know you weren't going to make it easy for her to go. And I think she thought this might be the best way for both of you."

Katrina didn't want to think rationally. She was in too much pain. "She was my world," Katrina muttered. "My all. I have nothing anymore."

"Ugh." Teri let out a moan that caused both women to look at her. "Look I'm sorry but I can't sit here and listen to this bullshit. Katrina, yes, you are hurting, yes, the woman you loved might have left. But you aren't going to sit here and act like she was all you have. Dude, Saura did what she felt was best, for both of you. Maybe she was wrong for her actions, but in the end you and I both know you weren't going to let her leave. May be you need to take a page from Saura's handbook and start focusing on yourself for a change. It's been a week; you still have on the same fucking clothes you had on when we went biking."

Katrina looked down at her athletic attire. She hadn't changed. The only things she had done for a week were go to the bathroom, eat, and drink.

"This isn't the end of the world, Tree," Devon added. "I know it might seem like it but think about it like this. This wasn't a bad breakup. She didn't cheat on you or something. This might not be the end. Maybe you both need this time apart to see if it is really what you want."

"All I want is Saura." Katrina sighed.

"Well what better way to get over this than going on your trip to Europe?" Devon smiled.

"Yeah, do you know how many fine-ass girls there are in Europe? Oh and think of the accents."

"Have your *Eat, Pray, Love* moment," Devon joked.

Katrina thought about what her friends were saying. If she had to get over her girl at least she wouldn't have to be in her house with all the memories haunting her every day. Katrina took a deep breath; she exhaled the negativity she had been harboring for Saura. She knew deep down that Saura only did what she did to protect them both. Although flawed, she knew she would have to get over her anger at some point; she just didn't know when that day would be.

Katrina walked her friends out. They were only willing to leave after they felt she was cheered up enough. She walked back in her empty house. She wondered would it ever feel like home again. Katrina noticed that one of the photos on the wall was missing. Obviously Saura had taken her favorite photo of them.

The house phone startled Katrina as it started to ring. The phone never rang and they only kept it because they had bad cell service in certain parts of the house. Katrina looked at the caller ID; it was an unknown number. Katrina's heart started to race. She picked up the phone and pressed talk.

"Katrina."

The voice sent chills down her spine. "Saura." Katrina fought to hold back all emotion.

"I'm sorry, Katrina. I know you are mad at me."

"Saura, why? We didn't even have a good-bye."

Saura wiped the tears falling from her eyes. "We did, the night before that last night we had. I didn't want to have a sad good-bye. If I would have stayed I don't think I would have been able to leave."

"That is incredibly selfish of you, Saura. Maybe I needed more. I wanted to have our last hug, our last kiss, and you robbed me of that."

"I am sorry. I hope you can forgive me one day."

Katrina wanted to yell and scream but she was too exhausted to do so. She didn't want to end on a bad note. Maybe if she left on good terms Saura would realize she belonged in Memphis with her. "I am hurt, but I will get over it. I want you to be happy, Saura."

"I want you to be happy too. You have no idea how much I want you to be happy." Saura tried to smile but couldn't.

There was a moment of silence as they both thought about what to say next.

"I love you, Saura. I wish you nothing but the best." Katrina couldn't believe she was able to say it.

Suddenly things didn't feel so bad. It was as if an anchor had been lifted off of her. She realized she actually meant it. Saura was the love of her life, and sometimes when you loved something you had to let it go. Saura didn't have a new number yet but she let Katrina know she unblocked her Facebook.

The two began to talk about Saura and the house. She was living in a house with seven other girls. Saura joked that it felt like she was on some reality show with a bunch of women all trying to do the same thing. Saura had met her agent who told her about jobs she submitted Saura for. Katrina couldn't help but notice the excitement in Saura's voice; she could tell she really was where she needed to be.

"I'm still going to Europe." Katrina cut Saura off while she was talking about one of the women in the house.

"That's great, you should still go." Saura shook her head trying to convince herself that she meant what she said.

"Yeah, I am going to go alone. I think I could use the time to myself."

There was another pause on the phone. Saura didn't know how she wanted to feel. The jealous girlfriend in her wanted to ask if Katrina planned on getting with anyone while she was there, but she knew she no longer had the right to ask those types of questions.

"I am sure you are going to have an amazing time. Take lots of pictures and eat lots of food." Saura struggled to keep her voice from trembling too much.

"I will."

The two hung up with each other. Katrina felt a sense of relief. She knew it would take time, but she knew time would heal all wounds. She didn't have time to focus on the sadness. She had a trip to prepare for.

Teri sat on her couch. She knew the time had come to cut Porsha off. Her usual cutoff lines didn't seem appropriate. Porsha hadn't done anything wrong. She never asked for money, or tried to show her off to her friends. She didn't have an advanced degree, but she was smart and out of all the women she had talked to, Porsha actually seemed like she might try to make something of herself one day.

Teri thought about Katrina. She and Saura were joined at the hip from the moment they met. She was surprised it lasted two years. Porsha was getting too comfortable in her house. She had to shut it down.

Teri couldn't think of anything to say. She didn't want the headache of answering a million questions as to why she didn't want to be with her anymore. She picked up her phone and pressed Porsha's name. Instead of pressing the phone button she pressed the little envelope on the phone.

Please don't be mad but I can't do this anymore. It's not you, it's me. I can't explain. I wish you luck in all your future endeavors. Teri

Teri pressed the send button, immediately regretting the decision to send a text instead of calling. Within seconds her phone rang. She pressed the ignore button only to have the phone ring back to back three times. On the final call her voicemail alert chimed. Teri didn't want to listen to it. Her phone chimed again as a text message came through.

Seriously, a text message! Well fuck you too then.

Teri knew she couldn't be mad. She knew the best thing was to spend a day or two at Devon's house. The last thing she needed was her white neighbors wondering why the black lesbian was causing a scene in their community.

As she got in her car she noticed a flyer for the daycare. Porsha popped in her head. She thought about all the amazing nights they shared and the meals she was going to miss. It almost made her want to call. But in the end she knew it was only right. It was always best to rip the Band-Aid instead of pulling it off slowly.

Teri pulled into her regular parking space at her job. She noticed a new car sitting in the spot reserved for the chief of staff of the hospital. She knew Carl had a love for cars but never expected to see him driving a cherry red sports car.

Teri greeted the nurses and staff as she headed to the pharmaceuticals department. Teri was the manager of the hospital's pharmacy and head pharmacist. The small hospital facility was created for terminally ill patients. Teri mostly dealt with high-end pharmaceuticals that were designed to make people's final days as comfortable as possible.

"Hey, Ming," Teri said as she walked into the main pharmacy area. The short Asian man was separating red pills into sets of four.

"What's up, boss?" Ming and Teri were the two pharmacists for the small hospital.

Teri was always amused by Ming and his need to try to talk as "urban" as he could. They joked around a lot about how Chinese his parents were and how they were pressuring him to marry someone. They had no idea that he was gay and currently in a long-term relationship with a buff black man who looked more like a football player than a doctor.

"What's the orders looking like?"

"Rather slow for right now. Did you see the new acting chief of staff yet?"

"New chief?" Teri turned around. "Where is Carl?"

"Gurl." Ming sat in his rolling chair and pushed himself across the floor. He crossed his legs and let the professional side completely go. "Do you not read your e-mail? Carl announced his resignation like two weeks ago. Haven't you noticed he hasn't been strutting around here?"

"I just figured he was off on one of his big trips."

Ming shook his head. "No, honey, he resigned. But you know I have the tea right? Baby told me that he had two sexual harassment claims filed by two of those little skanky nurses on the fourth floor. You know he was fucking them right?"

Teri curled her lips. It was a known fact that Carl had a thing for young, hot nurses. She had even walked past his office one day to hear moans coming from under the door.

"Well word on the floor is he had a wild night with the new blonde and that girl with the bad red hair color. So he tried to send a picture of his junk to one of their e-mails and made a mistake and included Ms. Harriett on the e-mail."

Teri's hand flew up over her mouth. "Get the fuck out of here!"

"Yes, ma'am." Ming threw his head back. "So you know that old bitty wasn't having it. So he resigned."

Teri laughed as she unlocked her office door.

"So anyway there's a new acting chief and the bitch is bad. Walked in here in a pair of red bottoms I would kill for."

There was a knock at the pharmacy door. One of the head office admins popped her head in. "Oh, Ms. Howard, you are here. They need you in a meeting in ten minutes in the conference room." The admin smiled before closing the door.

Teri and Ming looked at each other. The only time she was called into the big meetings was when big changes were being made.

Teri pressed the up button for the elevator. She got in the empty elevator and pressed the top floor.

"Can you hold that for me please?" a woman's voice rang out.

Teri quickly pressed the open button so the doors wouldn't close. Looking down, Teri noticed the tall black stilettos as they walked in the elevator. Teri's eyes shifted up as she admired the insanely sexy body of the chocolate woman with childbearing hips wearing a suit that looked like it was tailor made for her.

"Thank you," the woman replied. "Floor eight please." She smiled as she glanced over to see the button was already pressed. "Oh."

Teri and the woman made eye contact. Teri shifted in her position. She hadn't seen anyone that fine in a long time. The woman's chocolate skin looked completely flawless. Her hair was laid to perfection in a short, funky haircut, on her ears were obviously real diamonds, and there was no ring on the finger.

"Looks like we are headed in the same direction." Teri held her hand out. "I am Teri Howard."

The beauty shook Teri's hand. Her skin felt like silk. Teri noticed the change in expression when she said her name the woman's eyes widened.

"Ms. Howard, pharmacy right?"

"Yes, correct."

The woman shook Teri's hand faster. "I am Victoria Gold, the acting chief of staff."

"Oh yes, right, hello." Teri didn't want to let go of her hand. They finally stopped shaking hands as the elevator door opened to their floor.

"So I guess we are headed to the same place after all." Victoria chuckled.

"I guess so."

The two walked onto the administration floor. The receptionist sitting at the front desk looked at them as if she had seen a ghost. They smiled as they walked past her.

"She doesn't like me very much," Victoria whispered. "We had a small run-in this morning."

"Uh-oh, that doesn't sound good."

"Let's just say I like people to be prepared, and she wasn't."

They walked in the conference room to see all the department heads and board members sitting around the long conference table. Levi, the chair of the board, stood up.

“All right now it looks as though we can get started. As you all know Dr. Harrison is no longer with us. But we are pleased to introduce Dr. Victoria Gold as the acting chief of staff.”

The crowd all clapped as Victoria stood next to Levi. Victoria made eye contact with Teri briefly. A sexy smirk appeared on Victoria’s face. Teri couldn’t help but think that smirk was meant just for her.

“Well first I want to say it is wonderful to be here in Memphis. I come from Piedmont Healthcare in Atlanta, Georgia, but I have always loved the work that is being done in the healthcare world here in Memphis. I look forward to working with all of you.”

Teri scanned the room. Obviously she wasn’t the only one in awe of the new chief. Women were sizing her up while the men were trying to look through her clothes. Teri’s eyes made it back to Victoria. She was like everyone else; she couldn’t take her eyes off of her.

“Well I won’t hold any of you up. If you need anything my door is always open. Thank all of you again for your time.”

The room clapped again as people rushed to greet her and shake Victoria’s hand.

“Fine, isn’t she?” a deep voice whispered in Teri’s ear. Carlos, one of the doctors and Ming’s Adonis boyfriend, stood next to Teri.

“That she is,” Teri said admiring the way Victoria’s breasts seemed to be sitting up perfectly. She couldn’t help but wonder what they looked like.

“I think she bats for your team, too.”

Teri’s head quickly snapped around to Carlos. “Get out. What makes you think that?”

“Just a feeling I got when I met her this morning. She didn’t give me the look that most of these women around here do. You know, that ‘I will fuck the shit out of you’ look.”

Teri and Carlos both laughed. The room began to clear out. Victoria’s eyes shifted back to Teri. She began to walk toward Teri until she was standing in front of Carlos and Teri.

“Dr. Gold, this is—”

“Teri Howard. We met briefly in the elevator,” Victoria said cutting Carlos off. “And, please, call me Victoria.”

The intercom system rang out calling Carlos’s name.

“On that note I must get back to work.” Carlos nodded his head as he walked out the door.

“Well again it was nice meeting you, Teri. I am sure we will see lots of each other.”

Teri shrugged her shoulders. “I don’t know about that. They like to keep me locked away in the pharmacy.”

“Well we will have to do something about that.” Victoria winked.

Teri felt a familiar feeling creeping over her. She wondered if Victoria could be flirting with her.

“Well, let me go. You know they have me in meetings for the rest of the day. It was a pleasure meeting you, Teri. Until next time.”

Victoria walked out of the room leaving Teri standing in her spot. Teri shook her head; there was no way Victoria would be that bold on their first meeting. Teri chalked it up to her having an inviting personality as she headed back out of the room.

Chapter 4

Willow could tell the weather was about to take a turn for the worse when she dipped into her favorite small coffee shop. It was fairly empty; she knew the atmosphere would change as nighttime came and the famous SoHo area livened up with all kinds of characters. The one thing she loved about her holidays in the city was visiting the lesbian hangouts, something she didn't have near her university and definitely at her countryside home.

She ordered a cup of espresso and pulled out the book she was reading. She didn't know what made her listen to Piper who insisted that she read the latest mommy porn book that was sweeping the nation. She let herself get lost in the romance of the two main characters as best as she could in between the horrible writing. Willow shook her head as she read another repetitive statement from the male lead telling the female how much he loved her after screwing her brains out.

Within seconds of starting her book a loud clap of thunder rang out as large raindrops began falling to the ground. Willow loved the way the large raindrops were hitting the window of the coffee shop. It was calming; the perfect weather to get her through the bad book. Even through the bad parts, she felt a little envious of the main character. She wanted someone to long for her the way the male wanted the female in the book, just not with as many corny lines.

She buried her nose in the book. She heard the bell from the door ring out. Willow peeked up from her paperback to see a woman standing in the door. She nodded her head, as she watched the woman standing at the door trying to wipe the rain off her drenched outfit. Willow had to admit, the woman's choice of outfit was hot. The mix of preppy with a bit of urban flare was different from what she was used to out of the London lesbian scene. The woman's hair was braided in stylish cornrows in the front but loose braids in the back. She had to be at least five foot eleven, and very toned.

Willow watched as the woman shook her head. Willow felt her heart starting to race as she finally caught a glimpse of the woman's face. Not only could she dress but she had to be the sexiest butch woman she had ever seen in her life. Willow knew the book had warped her brain; she couldn't possibly be staring at someone as gorgeous as she thought.

"This rain stuff is crazy," the woman muttered as she looked out the window. She began scanning the coffee shop for a place to sit.

An American, Willow thought. No wonder she hadn't seen anyone like her before; she wasn't from London.

"I'm guessing you are new to London and our weather," Willow spoke out. She couldn't believe she actually said something to the woman.

The sexy specimen turned her head to the voice she just heard. Her eyes widened. There sat a beautiful chick staring at her. She wondered when she was going to see one of the London hot lesbians she'd seen pictures of online but up until then all she'd seen was white chicks or really butch black women. This girl was definitely different.

"Yeah, I knew it was called dreary London but this is ridiculous. It came out of nowhere." The woman walked closer to the table.

Willow smiled and nodded her head. "It happens. FYI: always carry an umbrella." Willow and the girl both laughed. Not only was she gorgeous but she had a beautiful smile to match. "Would you like to have a seat?" Willow asked.

The woman sat down at the empty chair at the small, round table. She put her carrier bag on the windowsill. "Hello, my name is Katrina, but most people call me Tree," Katrina said as she extended her hand.

Willow put her palm in Katrina's. She felt an electric pulse run through her body. Who was this girl and why was she having this effect on her? "I'm Willow; most people call me Willow." Willow smiled.

"That's cute." Katrina smiled back.

The two locked eyes again. Willow could feel her body heating up. Katrina was the most beautiful woman she had ever seen outside of television. Willow couldn't help wonder where the other half was. She knew someone that fine couldn't be single. "So what brings you to London?"

"Oh, food actually." Katrina glanced at the menu. "I'm a chef and I'm opening a restaurant in Memphis, Tennessee, so I decided to come over to Europe for a month to see the sights and taste the cuisine. I've been in London for three days; next up is Paris tomorrow."

Willow wanted to scream. The perfect woman walks in and sits at her table and she meets her on her final day. "Have you had anything good here?"

Katrina shrugged her shoulders. "Honestly, it's been okay. I am still wrapping my head around the fact that no one puts ice in drinks." They both laughed.

"Sorry to hear that. We have some great food places actually."

"Yeah, that's too bad. I've wanted something good but best I've found was fish and chips."

"Head over to Nando's and get some piri piri chicken." Willow batted her long natural eyelashes.

"Nando's? Yeah, I need to check that out. I love piri piri chicken," Katrina said not taking her eyes off Willow's big brown eyes.

The connection was obvious. The two chatted as if they were old friends catching up after a long time apart. They couldn't believe how much they had in common. Both loved food, traveling, and fashion. Willow told Katrina all about hot spots in various European countries she had visited. Katrina found herself admiring the well-traveled Willow. Although she could tell that Willow came from a certain type of wealth, she didn't come out like an arrogant rich chick.

"So if you love the countryside so much why are you even here in the big city?" Katrina asked Willow as she walked back to the table with two more coffees.

Willow's face dropped. She thought about her father. "Well after my father passed I decided to come back into the city and start working on my career again. I am a fashion designer."

"Really? Man, that's cool. I love fashion." Katrina nodded her head.

"I can tell; you have a very unique look about yourself. It was the first thing I noticed." Willow wanted to slap herself. She didn't want the girl thinking she was weird for staring at her.

"Really? Is unique a good thing or a bad thing?" Katrina asked.

"Good." Willow nodded her head. "Very good."

The two stared at each other smiling.

"So what brings you to London?" Willow took another sip of her coffee. She noticed the change in Katrina's face. Her face dropped a bit.

Katrina thought about Saura. “Well the truth is originally I was coming to try new foods and just experience being out of the country. But then my ex broke up with me and moved to another city so this trip became an experiment in healing.”

Willow wanted to jump for joy. At least the girl was single, which was all she needed to know.“I didn’t have a breakup, but when my father passed I just wanted to get back in the city to get away from our family home. Too many memories, ya know?” Willow sipped her coffee again.

“Yeah, I totally know.”

“Well, then, to escaping our pasts.” Willow held up her coffee cup.

“And to new futures.” Katrina clicked her cup against Willow’s. The intensity was growing; they couldn’t take their eyes off of each other. “So tell me more about this Nando’s place,” Katrina broke the silence.

“There’s one down the street actually. Best piri piri chicken you will ever eat.”

“Big words. I will have to check the place out. I do need to put something on my stomach other than coffee.”

Katrina and Willow both laughed. Three hours had passed and it felt like Katrina had just walked in. The rain had long passed and the nightlife of the street was starting to take over. The once empty coffee house was now buzzing with all sorts of characters, but somehow they still felt like they were the only ones in the room.

Katrina didn’t know what was coming over her but this girl was working a magic spell on her. She wasn’t ready to leave her just yet. “So, Ms. Willow, would you maybe like to introduce me to this Nando’s? I mean if you aren’t busy,” Katrina asked without taking her eyes off of Willow.

Willow felt the ball forming in the pit of her stomach. There weren't too many things she knew in life but one of them was that she wasn't going to let the night end in the coffee house.

"I guess I could eat." Willow smiled.

The two stood up, gathering their belongings. Katrina held the door for Willow. "Well, Ms. Willow, lead the way." Katrina held her arm out. Willow locked arms with Katrina, and she knew it wasn't going to be the last time.

The two walked out of the restaurant full on more than just food. They couldn't stop laughing and talking. Willow didn't know why, but it felt like she had known Katrina her whole life.

"So is there anything else you want to see in London?" Willow asked, still not wanting the night to end.

Katrina frowned as she shrugged her shoulders. "I don't think so, but I can say for the first time this whole time I don't want to leave."

Willow felt the butterflies flying in her stomach from Katrina's statement. She had to fight with herself to stay calm and not let her excitement cover her face.

"Well, there is one thing you have to do. I can't let you leave without doing one thing." Willow smiled as she held her arm out on the side of the street. A black cab pulled up in moments.

"What is the one thing?" Katrina questioned.

Willow smiled. "Don't you trust me?" Willow smiled as she opened the door to the cab.

Katrina thought about the question. She had known this girl for all of five hours and she was about to get in a funny-shaped car with her. "Strangely enough, yes, I do."

The cab drive just added to the amazing night. Willow pointed out all the sites, giving a brief synopsis of some of the buildings as they passed them. Katrina found herself regretting her decision as they arrived at the west bank. She stared at the massive London Eye Ferris wheel, the one thing she told herself she would never ride.

"Oh come on, you can't come to London and not ride the Eye." Willow chuckled as she took Katrina by her hand, pulling her along.

"See where I am from we tend to steer clear of places where we can fall to our death." Katrina's voice cracked.

"Trust me, you will love it."

The two grabbed tickets and got into the usually small line. Before they knew it they were in the capsule being closed in. Katrina held on to the rail, closing her eyes as tight as she could. Willow couldn't help but laugh, especially since there were children in their capsule who were super excited to make it to the top. Katrina squeezed Willow's hand as they started moving.

After a few minutes Willow tapped Katrina on her shoulder. "Can you do me a favor and just open your eyes for one moment?"

Katrina paused, but finally opened her eyes. The sight was breathtaking. The sun had set and the lights of London were illuminating the sky.

"Oh my God," Katrina said as she stared at the city that had treated her so poorly up until that day.

Willow continued to point out sites to Katrina as they went around. Finally they stopped at the top. Katrina looked over at Willow who was smiling while staring out the glass. Katrina didn't know what it was, but there was something special about this woman. She grabbed Willow's hand as their fingers interlocked.

The two headed back toward the street. The lights from the Ferris wheel shined off of the Thames River. The night was young and there were so many things to do just in that area alone. They headed down the dock to one of the river cruise boats. Willow pointed out sites as they cruised down the Thames River. After the ride Willow and Katrina walked hand in hand on South Bank until making it back to where the black cab originally dropped them off. It was the best either had felt in a long time.

"Well, Willow, thank you so much for this. You really have changed my opinion of this city."

Willow blushed. "I wish you had more time. There is so much more to show you. But you are going to love Paris. Don't forget to check out those places I told you about." Willow tried to think of something to keep Katrina with her, but she came up with nothing.

"Well maybe you could give me your number and I can call you when I get there, just to make sure I am remembering all the places. Do you have Facebook?"

Katrina held her phone out. They each exchanged phone numbers and Facebook usernames.

Two black cabs pulled up at the same time.

"I guess this is it. Thank you again, Ms. Willow," Katrina said as she held her arms out.

Katrina and Willow hugged. It felt like a magnet was holding them together. Finally they forced themselves to pull away.

Willow felt like she was floating. She opened the door to her flat to find Piper and Corrie sitting on her sofa drinking wine and watching television. She was so happy she didn't care that Piper was in the arms of Corrie, the ex she stated she wasn't going back to.

"And where have you been, miss?" Piper asked.

"Just having the best time of my life."

Piper and Corrie both noticed the grin on Willow's face.

"You slut, you met someone!" Piper jumped off the couch and ran up to her friend. "Tell me everything."

Willow could still see Katrina vividly in her mind. She could smell her cologne on her skin. "I met this girl named Katrina. Oh my God, she was gorgeous, intelligent, and sexy as hell."

Piper screeched.

Willow felt her iPhone buzzing in her pocket. She pulled it out to see the Facebook friend request notification. She quickly pressed accept and pulled up Katrina's profile photo. She held the phone out so Piper could see.

"Damn she is hot."

"Excuse me?" Corrie chimed in.

Piper shrugged her shoulders. "Sorry but she is. Why in the hell aren't you off shagging her?"

Willow sat down in one of her armchairs. "She is American. She's leaving for Paris in the morning."

"So!" Piper and Corrie said in unison.

"That's even more reason why you should be shagging her brains out right now." Piper folded her arms.

Willow shook her head. "Not everyone thinks about sex all the time." Willow rolled her eyes. "I wasn't trying to be some London fling, even if she was the perfect girl."

"Please, you could have shagged her so well she would say to hell with Paris."

Willow just shook her head while Piper and Corrie talked about all the things she should have been doing. She actually wished she had the balls to do the things they were saying; at least she would have still been with the American.

"So I need advice." Katrina fell down on her bed. She held her iPad up. Teri's face covered her iPad.

"Shoot," Teri said as she scrolled through Facebook on her computer.

"So I met this chick tonight and, Teri, I swear she was fucking amazing."

"You got some?" Teri's face quickly focused back on screen with Katrina's face.

"No, I didn't, but we spent practically the whole day together. She is gorgeous, funny. She was great."

"Sooo, why are you on Skype with me? Why aren't you deep in some London pussy right now?"

Katrina shook her head at her friend's vulgarity. "I'm leaving for Paris in the morning. As much as I wanted to, she seemed like she was better than just a one-night thing. I couldn't do it. I wanted to, but I couldn't. Damn she is fine. I'm looking at her Facebook right now."

"Oh, what's her name?"

Katrina told Teri the name, and she instantly looked Willow up. Katrina watched as Teri's eyes bulged until she finally turned back to her screen.

"Oh yeah, you are a fucking fool. Her legs would be wrapped around me right now."

Katrina thought about things for a moment. She didn't meet anyone in Amsterdam and hated London until that night. Now she finally met a girl to completely take her mind off of Saura and she let her go.

"Fuck I made a big mistake didn't I? Oh well I guess it's too late now."

Teri looked directly into the tiny camera on her computer. "It's never too late for pussy. And even if it is, don't you have two train tickets to Paris?"

"What are you saying?"

"I'm saying you are in Europe, live a little." Teri winked.

Katrina told Teri she would call her back. She stared at Willow's profile photo. Teri's voice echoed in her head. She was supposed to be having adventures and up until now all she did was look at famous monuments, eat, and take selfies. She noticed Willow's Skype name was on her profile. She typed it in and saw that she was online. Katrina took a deep breath and pressed call.

Willow sat in the chair watching the movie with Piper and Corrie. Her phone began to ring. She picked it up to see she had a Skype call coming in from Katrina.

"Oh my God it's her!" Willow yelled as she sat up. "What do I do?"

"Answer it!" Piper and Corrie said together.

Willow took a deep breath and pressed answer. A moment later Katrina's face appeared on her phone.

Katrina took a deep breath. "Hey um, this might sound crazy as hell but if I have a week in Paris and an extra train ticket. Would it be incredibly crazy of me to ask you to join me?"

Willow's heart skipped a beat. She held on to her phone while biting her lip. Just earlier that morning she had plans on spending the week locked in her flat reading the horrible book and sketching ideas. Now she had an invitation to go to the most romantic city in the world with a beautiful stranger.

Piper and Corrie were both motioning for her to say yes but her mind was screaming no. Everything about this seemed like a bad TV movie in the making. No matter the connection, the truth was she didn't know Katrina at all, and hopping on a train and spending a week with the gorgeous stranger had to be a bad idea.

"Do you mind holding for one moment?"

"Sure," Katrina said nervously.

Willow pressed the mute button.

"Girl, go!" Piper yelled. "Are you mental? You have to go."

"I don't know this woman."

"You don't know anyone until you get to know them. Why not get to know her in Paris with a free ticket?" Corrie added her two cents.

"Willz, listen to me, honey." Piper got up. She sat on her knees in front of Willow. "Your life is incredibly boring. Seriously I don't understand how you live like this. For once you have the chance to experience a real adventure. Get all her information so I have it, and take your ass to Paris."

Willow looked at her best friend. She thought about the offer. It was insane to even consider it, let alone actually go. Willow took a deep breath and held her phone back up. She pressed the mute button again.

"Well what kind of person would I be if I left the American to fend for herself in a city she knows nothing about?" Willow smiled.

It was a bad idea, but she didn't care. She was going to Paris.

Chapter 5

"Are you ready?"

"I don't think I will ever be ready," Katrina said nervously.

The two stood at the bottom of the Eiffel Tower. The blissful week had passed by as soon as it started. The two spent days walking the streets of Paris, admiring its beauty, and tasting its famous cuisine. The couple would spend the mornings exploring French markets. Willow loved watching Katrina when she was around food. Katrina's face lit up like a kid at Christmas when they made it to the Marché Maubert marketplace. Katrina didn't eat; she studied the various market fare, taking time to ask questions. She taught Willow the differences between textures and tastes. Willow was in awe. Katrina talked about food the way an artist talked about art.

Katrina was equally impressed by Willow. She spoke French, which came in handy for Katrina who couldn't understand anything people were saying. Willow showed her all the famous sites. They spent one whole day getting lost in the Louvre and another day playing tourist wearing berets while riding the hop-on hop-off bus.

The best time of all was nighttime. Paris came to life at night. Lights twinkled on trees and bridges. Katrina understood why it was called the City of Lights; there were thousands all helping to create the most romantic atmosphere ever. Willow loved sitting on benches just talking about all kinds of things with Katrina. They felt like they had known each other forever. Before they knew it the week had come to an end.

"It's the last day, Katrina; you have to do it now."

Katrina stared at the tall tower. She was terrified of going to the top. Willow couldn't help but laugh.

"This just seems like a horrible idea," Katrina mumbled.

"You said the same thing about the Eye and it wasn't that bad. Come on don't you trust me by now?"

Katrina looked at Willow's innocent face. She shook her head as she walked past Willow toward the Eiffel Tower entrance.

The top was breathtaking. Katrina couldn't believe how small everything looked from the top. Willow held on to Katrina's hand. Katrina had given her the best week of her life. If nothing else she knew she had a friend she would never forget.

The sun setting set the most beautiful scene. Willow snapped photos with her phone. Katrina took a moment from admiring the scene to admire the woman standing right next to her. She had an amazing week and once again it was coming to an end. Willow felt Katrina's eyes on her; she turned her face toward Katrina who was staring directly at her.

"What's wrong?" Willow asked Katrina who just continued to stare.

Katrina wrapped her arm around Willow and pulled her into her body. She pressed her lips against Willow's lips. Willow's body tensed for a moment before she put her arms around Katrina, accepting the kiss by kissing her back in return. Willow parted her lips allowing Katrina to slip inside. Willow didn't know if it was the magic of the city, but it was the best kiss she had ever had. Katrina's soft lips felt so good, causing Willow's body to quiver from ecstasy. Katrina placed her hand on the back of

Willow's head allowing her fingers to get lost in Willow's curly mane. It didn't matter that other people were on the floor with them; the only thing that mattered was them and that moment. Neither wanted it to end, but finally it did.

"Well, that was unexpected." Willow tried not to blush too hard.

"I have wanted to do that since the London Eye," Katrina said still not taking her eyes off the beauty in front of her.

"Why now?"

"Because I needed to find a way to get you to come with me to Rome." Katrina smirked.

Willow felt her body heating up again. She secretly hoped she would get an invitation for the next destination. "Are you sure you aren't getting tired of me yet?"

Katrina shook her head. "Nah, I need to be able to kiss you in the Coliseum, too."

Katrina and Willow couldn't keep their hands off of each other. They made out in the cab that took them back to their room, completely not caring about the cab driver. Willow wanted nothing more than to give herself to Katrina.

They opened the door to the room. Katrina pushed Willow against the door as it closed. She kissed her on her neck, nibbling at her right earlobe. Willow pressed her knee against Katrina's pelvis as Katrina pulled Willow's shirt over her head. Katrina admired Willow's breasts that were sitting perfectly in her lace bra.

Katrina's tongue slowly ran down Willow's right breast while massaging the left one. Willow's nipples stood at attention waiting for Katrina to take them. She obliged, licking circles around the rock-hard brown nipple until pressing her lips against it. Willow let out a sigh of pleasure.

There were no words spoken. They kissed until finding the bed. Willow unbuckled Katrina's jeans and pulled them down to her feet. Katrina pulled her shirt over her head right before Willow pushed her to the bed. The aggressive side of Willow shocked Katrina. As the stud she was used to being in control sexually. Willow didn't care; she pulled Katrina's boxer briefs down.

"Hold on, you don't run this," Katrina said in an attempt to establish dominance.

"Oh yeah?"

Willow ignored the statement as she pushed Katrina's legs open. Willow's tongue parted Katrina's walls, devouring her.

Katrina mouth dropped open but words didn't escape, only a moan for more. Although she loved getting head, she didn't get it often. Most femmes she dated ended up being pillow princesses she didn't allow to go down on her. Saura was the only woman who had tasted Katrina before.

Willow didn't realize how starved for sexual attention she was. She felt completely ravenous, devouring Katrina. Katrina bit her lip. She didn't know head could feel so good. Saura always loved giving her head, but it felt nothing like this. In that moment she was Willow's bitch, and she didn't care.

Willow didn't feel like herself anymore; another person had taken over her body as she buried her face deep into the depth of Katrina. She felt Katrina's legs wrap around her. Before she knew it Katrina used her lower body strength to push her over on her back. Katrina sat on top of her. She pushed Willow's hands down the bed over her head.

Katrina sucked on Willow's nipples, not letting her move from the pinned position she had her in. Her tongue traced down from her breasts to her stomach. She left small passion marks on her stomach as a reminder of who was in charge.

Katrina moved down Willow's body until she reached her softest place. With her index finger she entered Willow and pulled it back out covered in Willow's wetness. She sucked Willow's nectar off of her finger and shook her head.

"I knew you were going to taste good," Katrina purred as she lowered her body.

She parted Willow, not wanting to start easy; she stuck her tongue deep into Willow tongue fucking her into a frenzy. Willow covered her eyes; it was the most amazing feeling she had ever felt. Katrina did things to her she didn't know were possible. Katrina's fingers entered her while she sucked on Willow's clit.

Willow felt like she was going to die. The pleasure was killing her slowly. She knew Katrina had to be from another planet; no mere human could do the things she was doing to her body. Katrina felt Willow throbbing against her fingers. Willow's pussy tightened against her fingers until a flood of nectar trickled out. Katrina smiled, as Willow fought to catch her breath from the orgasm consuming her body.

Willow submitted to Katrina's every will. Their bodies pressed against each other as they ground in unison. Katrina ran her fingers through Willow's hair while Willow's fingers dug into Katrina's back. They worked their bodies faster and faster until reaching the ultimate heights. They exploded together while their tongues danced the forbidden dance together.

There were no words. They looked at each other as their bodies lay intertwined together. Katrina kissed Willow on her forehead causing butterflies to fill Willow's stomach. With a final kiss the couple fell asleep for the last time in the most romantic city on earth.

Chapter 6

Devon threw her leg up on an empty bench. Jogging on the riverfront was becoming her favorite thing to do. She stretched her muscles after her two miles and her run up and down a set large set of steps that most people tried to avoid. The Memphis humidity was brutal; she grabbed a cool cloth and put it on the back of her neck.

"Need any help?"

Devon froze. The familiar voice still haunted her dreams at night. She didn't want to turn around, but she couldn't resist. Standing behind her was her ex, Shanice. She wanted to scream; not only was she standing there in the flesh, but she looked amazing. The short jogging shorts gripped her thin, long legs and the fitted tank hugged her little breasts, which were obviously missing a bra.

"Hi." Devon quickly put her shades on her face.

"I can't believe you are here." Shanice wrapped her arms around Devon.

Against her better judgment, Devon hugged her back. "Neither can I; aren't you supposed to be in Atlanta?"

Shanice moved to Atlanta three years earlier with the girl she left Devon for, again. It wasn't the first time Shanice had traded Devon in for a new face. Devon hadn't been to black gay pride in Atlanta since, just because she didn't want to run into her.

"I just moved back about a month ago. I was going to call you but, well I didn't want to get cursed out." Shanice flashed her smile. Devon could tell she had work done on her mouth.

"Well, welcome back. I gotta run." Devon turned away.

"Hey, Dev," Shanice called out.

Devon wanted to scream. She knew she needed to get away and fast. She turned around and flashed the fakest smile she could manage.

"Look there are some things I'd really like to talk to you about. Is it okay if I call you sometimes?"

Hell no, bitch, don't ever call my fucking phone! The words ran through Devon's head but she couldn't make them actually come out of her mouth.

"My number hasn't changed. I gotta go." Devon put her ear buds in her ear, turned around, and ran off. She heard Shanice call her name but acted like she couldn't hear over the sound of the nonexistent music coming from her ear buds.

Devon leaned against her car the moment she made it back to it. Her heart was racing. The last thing she needed was Shanice back in Memphis.

Suddenly office meetings weren't so boring anymore. Teri couldn't take her eyes off of Victoria. She had to force herself to concentrate instead of dreaming about all the things she could do to Victoria. She had already fantasized about sex in every private area she knew of in the hospital, including her office.

Teri searched Victoria's body for a flaw. She knew she had to have one, but it just couldn't be seen. This made her want to see her naked even more. The thing bothering her more than ever was the bad reading she was getting on her internal gaydar. Usually Teri could easily pick out a lesbian, bisexual, or curious chick, but with Victoria she was drawing a blank.

Teri thought about just trying her luck but knew that was a terrible idea. The last thing she needed or wanted was a sexual harassment complaint for telling someone they looked attractive. She worked hard to keep her personal life outside of the job. The only people who knew her sexual orientation were Ming and his mate. Although there were tons of cute nurses and aides who flirted with her all the time, she steered clear.

Victoria said something that made everyone laugh, bringing Teri back from her fantasy world. Teri joined in the clapping as the managers began to stand up. Carlos walked up to Teri; he stood next to her with his back to the wall.

"So when you gon' try to get that?" his deep voice muttered.

"Shut up, and we don't know if she is or isn't."

"I bet you lunch she is." Carlos smiled and nodded his head at one of the admins who had a huge crush on him.

"Whatever." Teri shook her head.

"Ms. Howard," Victoria called out startling Carlos and Teri.

Teri said good-bye to Carlos as he waved at Victoria. Teri and Victoria were the only ones left in the room. Teri couldn't help but laugh, as that was the same start to a few of her sexual fantasies about Victoria. She walked toward the front as Victoria gathered her belongings.

"Hello Ms. Gold, great meeting," Teri said in her most professional voice.

"Yeah, right, I hate these things." Victoria ran her hand through her bouncy hair. "That's actually why I needed you. I know this might be asking a lot but could you possibly hook a sista up with some pills? I have the worst headache."

Teri winced. "Um, is this a setup? Are you trying to get rid of me for giving you drugs?"

"I could write a prescription if you like." Victoria looked at her with a blank expression.

Teri stood for a moment trying to figure out if she was joking. Victoria continued to stare for a moment before a huge smile covered her face.

"I'm just fucking with you," Victoria jested, playfully hit Teri on her arm. "Lighten up, Teri."

Teri didn't know what to make of Victoria. She still couldn't tell if she was gay, but she obviously had a wild side. Teri just wondered how wild she could get.

"Hey with the way things go around here a person has to be extra careful, but it's not a problem. The hospital actually has me keep extra in case a nurse ever needs one, which is often."

"Great, well I'll send my assistant to come and get it from you." Victoria walked away, answering her phone as she disappeared out of the room, leaving Teri completely intrigued by the beautiful doctor.

Chapter 7

It was a short plane ride and the couple found themselves in the Eternal City, Rome. Katrina was already excited, but seeing the love and enthusiasm Willow had for the city delighted Katrina. They didn't waste time; after checking into their hotel they headed out to rent a scooter.

Katrina was terrified as she sat on the back of Willow's scooter. She felt like her life was going to end in Rome as Willow zoomed past cars and down alleys. The terror subsided as she admired the city. It was the perfect mix of old and new. Historical ruins sat next to Italian restaurants and cafés. Katrina couldn't believe her eyes as they pulled up to the Coliseum and parked the scooter in an area with a bunch of other ones.

"Hey do you want to put your money stuff in my money pouch? I hear the pickpocketing is really bad out here." Katrina surveyed the area around them.

"Oh yeah, it's pretty bad; you better keep that thing close." Willow smirked.

"All right, don't be looking at me when your passport comes up missing."

Katrina noticed the confused expression on Willow's face.

"Why would you bring your passport?" Willow questioned.

Katrina realized it was dumb of her to bring her passport. She stuffed it in the money pouch she bought, burying it deep under her clothes and against her chest.

"Keep walking, ignore them." Willow grabbed Katrina's hand as they whisked past a group of men aggressively trying to sell them scarves. They were relentless in their pursuits and the moment they made it past the first group another group selling other random trinkets appeared. It only took a few moments of men shoving crap in their faces for Katrina to have enough. Things changed the moment she was clear of the men and able to truly take in that she was standing in front of a monument she had dreamed of seeing her whole life.

The Coliseum was breathtaking. Katrina stood outside admiring the massive ancient amphitheatre. Willow turned around when she realized Katrina wasn't walking beside her anymore. She ran back to Katrina who was in awe of the building.

"When I was a kid I was obsessed with Greek and Roman mythology. I watched *Hercules* and *Xena* faithfully every day when I got home from school. Recently the new show *Spartacus* became my favorite show on television." Katrina continued to stare at the structure. "I can't believe I am actually standing here."

"Well wait until you are standing inside." Willow smiled. "Come on you rebel, follow your Domina."

Katrina was impressed. Willow obviously watched the same show she did by her use of the lingo. Willow led Katrina up the stairs. She put her hands over Katrina's face and guided her to a platform.

"Ready?" Willow said as Katrina nodded her head.

Willow moved her hands. Katrina's mouth fell open as she overlooked the inside of the Coliseum. Sunrays shined down illuminating the green grass that peered through the massive columns of brick that created entryways and rail systems back in the day.

"This is fucking amazing." Katrina admired the massive arena.

"I stayed here for a month once, and every day I would come admire the beauty of this place. I love the way the sun peeks through each archway."

Katrina held Willow's hand as the two stood in silence just existing in the moment.

After the Coliseum they hopped back on the scooter. They took a stop at the Church of Santa Maria where Katrina stuck her hand in the Mouth of Truth. After passing countless beautiful fountains they allowed themselves time to wander around the Roman Forum. Exhausted, they headed back to the room where Willow fell asleep in Katrina's arms. When they finally woke up it was dark outside.

"Okay, I'm starving." Katrina rubbed her stomach.

"Oh I know exactly where we should go."

They caught a cab as Willow spoke Italian to the driver. They pulled up to an area filled with tourists. Katrina's stomach rumbled at the smell of garlic coming from some of the cafés. They grabbed a table at a beautiful little café. Katrina took over, ordering pasta dishes for both of them.

"So why is this place so busy?" Katrina watched as a tour group walked passed them.

"You will find out soon enough."

Katrina pulled her phone out, making notes about the food she ordered, snapping photos of their dishes and dessert as they came out. Willow was taken by how Katrina didn't just eat, she savored her food. She explained the textures of the wine they drank, showing Willow the proper way to smell and sip wine.

"That was amazing." Katrina handed her credit card and the bill to the waiter. "I swear I just want to go back to the room and go back to sleep."

"Not yet." Willow grinned. "We have one other thing to see while we are over here."

Willow took Katrina by her hand as they rushed past tourists and more men selling knickknacks. Katrina could hear something that sounded like a waterfall. Willow stopped causing Katrina to knock into her. She turned around smiling from ear to ear at Katrina.

"Okay, so the final thing of our night is right around this corner."

"Okay, what are you up to?"

"Katrina, welcome to the *Fontana di Trevi*."

The couple walked as the illuminated fountain came into view. People sat on the steps; some cuddled up while others snapped photos of friends and family standing in front of the large fountain. The duo headed down the steps until they were standing directly in front of the fountain. Katrina snapped photos with her phone, but realized none truly captured the beauty of the fountain.

After taking selfies with Katrina, Willow grabbed Katrina's hand. She placed two coins in her hand.

"So I'm supposed to throw these in?" Katrina looked at the fifty cent Euro coins.

"Don't you know the myth?"

"No, enlighten me." Katrina rubbed the coins together.

"Well the saying goes that you are supposed to throw two coins in. The one is to ensure you are going to come back to Rome, and the second is so you can find love or get married."

Saura's face appeared in Katrina's head. The last thing she wanted was to fall in love again. "I think I only need to throw one then." Katrina turned her back toward the fountain.

Katrina threw the first coin over her left shoulder. Willow clapped as the coin hit the illuminated water. Katrina noticed how the dim lights and the illumination from the fountain lights put a soft glow on Willow's face. There was something special about the Brit. She didn't know if it was being in the Eternal City, or the romantic feel of the Trevi but Katrina felt a calm she hadn't had in a while.

"You know what? What the hell," Katrina said as she threw the second coin over her shoulder.

Chapter 8

Willow sat on her exercise ball with a frown on her face. She watched as Katrina packed her suitcase. Each shirt was ironed and rolled with a precision Willow couldn't understand. Whenever she packed her bags she just folded items and worried about the wrinkles when she arrived at her destination.

"If you're going to stare at me, how about not looking like a sad puppy dog?" Katrina smirked.

The edges of Willow's mouth turned down as far as she could manage. She stuck her bottom lip out and folded her arms like a child. The pathetic excuse for pouting only made Katrina laugh harder.

Having such an amazing time together the couple decided they didn't want to part after Rome. After Rome they headed to Naples, hiked Mount Vesuvius and admired and explored the ancient city of Pompeii. Katrina let go of her fears during a day trip to Positano where they jumped off cliffs into the beautiful water and swam in the mysterious caves off the Amalfi coast. Their final stop was the City of Water, Venice, where they spent the nights getting lost down the Venice alleys or enjoying a romantic gondola ride. Not ready to leave, Willow talked Katrina into spending two more weeks in London with her. She introduced her to Piper who insisted they were meant for each other.

"Sleeping is going to suck without you," Willow said as she stared at her bed; she really didn't want to go back to sleeping alone. She knew it was time for Katrina to get back home. Her friend Devon had been calling her daily about the restaurant that was ready to open whenever she arrived.

"I can tell you I am not looking forward to my bed at home either," Katrina gazed up from her suitcase to see Willow's face etched completely with pain. Things hadn't gone the way she planned. Having some casual flings with hot European girls was on her bucket list, not meeting one amazing woman. She knew this feeling well, except this time she was the one leaving. In her mind she knew the truth: she had totally fallen for her British beauty.

Willow knew she was in trouble. In one month she had fallen irrevocably in love with the American. She wanted to tell Katrina the truth, but what would that help? She was getting on a plane in a little more than twenty-four hours. Their wild romance had come to an end.

"So what happens now?" Willow forced herself to mutter the phrase they had been avoiding since getting back to London.

Katrina sighed; as much as she wanted to believe that things could work, she knew the truth. Although the month was the most amazing time of her life, she had just gone through a breakup and the last thing she wanted to do was hurt Willow. If she couldn't make a relationship work with Saura who was only on the other side of the US, how could she even attempt to make something work with the girl she had only known for a month across the pond?

"Willow, I really don't know how to answer that." Katrina took a seat on the side of the bed.

There was an awkward silence in the room. They both knew the answer; there was no need to ruin the little bit of time they had left.

"Hey." Katrina stood up. "It's early, let's go do something."

Willow's eyes brightened for the first time the whole day. "Go where?"

"I don't know; somewhere. It's our last day together; we might as well go out with a bang." Katrina snapped her fingers. "I got it!"

Willow watched as a big smile covered Katrina's face.

"We have some unfinished business."

A short train ride later the two found themselves standing on the Pont des Arts bridge. Willow watched as lovers hugged while locking their locks on the famous bridge. The Seine that usually looked dirty to her when she usually visited Paris now had a beauty to it she never noticed before.

"Okay, so how does this work?" Katrina said fidgeting with the plastic the lock came in.

"I can't believe we are doing this. You have a flight to catch in a few hours and we are here in Paris."

"Hey, what's the worst that can happen? I miss my flight? That wouldn't be so bad." Katrina scooped Willow into her arms, spinning her around.

Willow never wanted the moment to end. She wrote their initials on the lock. They found an empty spot next to a light post.

"So, Willow, tell me what do we do now?" Katrina asked as she wrapped her arms around Willow.

Willow sighed as she felt the warmth of Katrina's breath against the nape of her neck. "If we lock this on the bridge and throw the key in the river it symbolizes that you are locking your heart away for the other person."

Katrina held Willow's hand. "Willow, I just want you to understand that I have never felt like this before. You are an amazing woman and you made this trip something I will never forget." Katrina pecked Willow on her lips.

Willow pressed down on the lock until they both heard a faint click. She pulled on the lock, but it didn't budge.

Willow turned around to Katrina as she took the key out of her pocket.

“I never want to forget this, or you,” Katrina whispered in Willow’s ear. Their lips drew closer as she dropped the key into the Seine. Neither wanted the moment to end.

The two held hands the entire two-hour ride back to London. Willow rested her head against Katrina’s shoulder. Katrina ran her hand through Willow’s wild, curly tresses. For once in life Willow despised time. She prayed that Father Time would slow down for once in life just so that she didn’t have to be without Katrina, but with every moment they drew closer to London, and closer to the end. It would never be the same again.

The couple exited the train and headed to the Tube never letting go of each other’s hands. The lateness was a pleasure as the underground subway wasn’t nearly as busy as it usually was. Katrina put her arm around Willow, kissing her on her forehead.

“I swear there is one thing I am not going to miss,” Katrina said as a train zipped past them.

“Yeah, yeah, yeah, you probably aren’t going to miss anything about my city.”

“Not true. I actually like London now.” Katrina held on to Willow. “Plus this city introduced me to you, so I really love it.”

The two laughed as their train approached. The car was mostly empty. The couple sat next to each other. Willow noticed the time on her cell phone. They had four more hours before she had to get Katrina to the airport. She didn’t want to waste another minute.

Willow pressed her lips against Katrina’s neck. Katrina laughed as she attempted to question what Willow was doing in the subway. Willow rubbed her hand on Katrina’s thigh, slowly moving farther in until reaching her inner thigh. Katrina turned her head to Willow. Their eyes locked. In that moment nothing mattered.

Their lips locked. Each wanted nothing more than to savor the taste of each other. Katrina's fingers gripped the back of Willow's head through her curls. She aggressively pulled Willow's face as close as she could get it. They kissed, breathing love and passion into each other.

The couple only broke the embrace once the train arrived at their stop. They rushed to the flat they shared. As soon as Katrina got the door open it was on. With one quick pull Katrina ripped Willow's dress into two pieces. Willow didn't care about the shattered fabric; she wanted Katrina more than she had ever wanted anything in life. Katrina circled her tongue around Willow's hard, light brown nipples. Katrina cupped Willow's ass, pulling her as close as she could. They walked slowly until making it into the bedroom.

Willow watched as Katrina took her clothes off. Katrina's ripped, sexy body caused the stiffness of Willow's nipples to ache from anticipation of what was to come. She didn't want to wait for her to take her clothes off; every moment was time she was missing touching her, caressing her, tasting her.

"Tree, take me. Please, I need you," Willow whimpered.

Katrina obliged pulling her foot out of her jeans. She towered over Willow, pulling Willow's legs toward her. Heat pulsated between Willow's legs; her whole body trembled. Katrina's touch electrified every inch of Willow's body. Each touch only intensified until Willow's body felt like it was going to explode.

Katrina dove in, pressing her lips against Willow's swollen clit. Her tongue parted Willow, tasting the salty and sweetness of the woman who was once just a stranger in a coffee house. It was her favorite taste and she didn't know if she would ever taste her again. Katrina wanted to savor Willow; she wanted Willow to remain in her taste buds for those nights she wouldn't be able to have her again.

Willow bit her lip and placed her hand over her eyes. Katrina was putting a hurting on her in the most pleasurable way ever. The mix of tongue, lips, and the vibrating of Katrina's tongue felt better than any sexual contraption ever could.

"I need to be inside you," Katrina whispered.

Willow's eyes tightened closed as Katrina's fingers entered her. If she bit her lip any harder she would break skin. Katrina quickly found her G-spot, already completely familiar with all the inner workings of Willow's softest places. Flashes of their relationship played like a film in her head. Willow could hear the bell from the coffee house door ringing in her head.

They didn't close their eyes. Both stared at each other as stroke after stroke brought them closer to the pleasurable death. Willow had never felt so good. Her heat and wetness covered Katrina's hand. Katrina wanted to go as deep as she could, touching all the inner pleasure points Willow's body would allow. Katrina knew it might be the end, but she didn't want Willow to think it. She wanted Willow to feel her for the rest of her life.

Willow's body tensed as the erotic death was creeping upon her. She stared deeply into the eyes of the woman who had stolen her heart in just a month. Hitting her spots her body began to tremble until trembles turned into jerks. She exploded as Katrina held inside, exploding with her love. The river flowing from between Willow's thighs matched the river of tears flowing down her face. Willow jumped out of the bed and ran into her bathroom.

"Willow!" Katrina jumped up but Willow closed the door before she could make it to her.

Willow didn't want Katrina to see her cry. She hated what was happening. She wanted to curse everything that was taking Katrina away from her.

"Just give me a moment." Willow forced herself to sound as normal as possible.

Katrina knew that Willow was crying. She knew that Willow was crazy about her, and she was crazy about Katrina. Katrina didn't know what was keeping her together. Maybe it was Saura and the fact that she had just gone through the same thing. She couldn't believe she allowed herself to get into another impossible situation.

Willow fixed her face as much as she could before coming out of the bathroom. Katrina was sitting on the side of the bed. Willow forced a smile as she crawled back into the bed.

"I am sorry, Willow."

"Sorry for what?"

"For causing you this pain. I know how it feels to watch someone leave you. I hate that I have put you in this position."

Willow wrapped her arms around Katrina's back. "Katrina, don't feel like that. We are both adults who just had an amazing time together. I will never forget this month and I hope you won't either. But in the end I am happy to just have been able to spend this time with you. It's something I needed, we both needed."

Katrina turned her face toward Willow. She put her hand on Willow's right cheek. There was something so special about her; she was genuine. It was refreshing. Time was gone, it was time to say goodbye, yet neither wanted to pull away from each other.

Chapter 9

"You have everything?"

The couple stood at the United Airlines check-in at Heathrow Airport. Katrina held Willow's hand while they waited for a kiosk to open up.

"Yeah, I do. Hey I locked Devon's number in your phone in case you need it. I will call you when I get home."

An open kiosk opened and Katrina punched in her info and scanned her passport. Willow watched as Katrina grabbed her boarding pass.

"I guess this is it then." Willow smiled. She didn't know how she was able to smile but she managed one.

"Yeah, I guess so. No tears, my weeping Willow." Katrina caressed Willow's cheek.

"No tears," Willow said as she felt the tears forming in her eyes.

Katrina pulled Willow close planting a long kiss against her forehead. "Talk to you later," Katrina said as she walked off. She didn't want to turn around. She knew if she turned around she might not leave.

Willow watched the woman she was crazy about disappear into the crowd. It was over as quickly as it started. She didn't feel like taking the Tube home so she grabbed a black cab. Suddenly everything reminded her of Katrina. She smiled as she passed different things that they went to, remembering the fun they had.

Willow arrived back at her home to find Piper trying on a dress that she was in the process of making.

"Okay, first off this dress has to belong to me. And second off, how you holding up, honey?"

Willow sat on her couch, Piper joined her.

"I can't believe it's over. Hell I can't believe it happened to begin with." Willow sighed.

Piper put her hand on Willow's thigh. "The good thing is that now you know." Piper smiled.

"I know what? That life isn't fair?"

"No, that the real thing is out there; you just have be open to it."

Willow turned her face toward her friend. "But what if I just let the one get on a plane to America?"

The two sat in silence pondering the question. Piper suddenly jumped up. "Okay, I have one question: why didn't you go to America with her?"

Willow shrugged her shoulders. She had thought about that question a million times. Katrina never asked her to come to the States even though they had joked about her coming and visiting Graceland. In the end a wild European vacation was one thing, but Willow packing up and heading to America just seemed farfetched for some reason.

"Well I do have a career to think about, and she has a restaurant about to open."

"Um, I'm sorry but is your sewing machine attached to the floor?"

"What?" Willow looked at her friend who was looking at herself in the full-length mirror.

"I'm just saying, you work from home, you can sketch and create clothes anywhere."

Willow knew Piper was right. "She didn't ask me to come. If she wanted me in America she would have asked just like she asked me to travel with her."

"I guess." Piper pulled the half-finished dress off and threw her little dress over her head. "Anywho, I gotta get out of here so I can go to work. Let's hang later."

Willow nodded her head. She got up and locked the door behind her. She thought about Piper's questions. Maybe she should have offered to come. Did she miss the chance to be with the woman she couldn't stop thinking about? Willow shook her head trying to shake the thoughts out as well. She knew wondering would drive her crazy. She picked up the dress that Piper had tried on. At least she could throw herself into her work; that was something that could take her mind off of Katrina, at least for a little bit.

Chapter 10

Katrina slept the majority of her flight. She had the layover from hell in Chicago when her flight was delayed due to late flight attendants. She couldn't jump out of her seat fast enough when the pilot announced they could get up to get off the plane.

The Memphis International Airport left much to be desired after being in Heathrow. There weren't stores all over the place, just a few places to eat and a Hudson newsstand. Katrina never noticed how bare the walls were in the Memphis airport. In the end it didn't matter. She was happy to be home.

Devon pulled into the airport baggage claim and pickup area. She answered her phone as it started to ring.

"Are you there yet?" Teri's voice echoed through the speakers in Devon's car.

"Pulling up now, I'll call you when I see he . . . Ahhhh!"

Devon screamed when two hands hit her driver's side window. Standing there was Katrina with a big, goofy smile on her face.

"This bitch right here!" Devon cursed, something she tried not to do too often.

"What happened?" Teri questioned.

"I'm going to kill Katrina." Devon opened her door. "I fucking hate you now."

Devon got out of the car and hugged Katrina who couldn't stop laughing. Devon playfully punched Katrina on her arm. Katrina put her stuff in the back seat and ran to the passenger side as the airport officer blew his whistle alerting them that they needed to move.

“What the hell is happening over there?” Teri’s voice echoed through the car again.

“Hey, Teri. I scared the shit out of Devon,” Katrina said still laughing.

“Ha ha ha, so funny.” Devon threw her middle finger at Katrina.

“What’s up homie, welcome home,” Teri said.

“Thanks, I’m just ready to get home and get some rest.”

“Not too much rest; we have work to do,” Devon added.

Katrina told them about her final days in London on the drive home. She found herself talking mostly about Willow and the amazing things she showed her in London.

“So, Tree, why didn’t you invite her to come to Memphis with you?”

Katrina shrugged her shoulders. She thought about that the majority of the plane ride. “I thought about it, but seriously we just spent time in some of the most amazing places in the world. How can we go from Rome to Memphis?”

“Hey there is nothing wrong with Memphis. People come from all over the world to come here,” Teri said. She was always quick to take up for the city that she loved.

“Yeah, Tree, and just because it’s not new to you doesn’t mean she wouldn’t be interested in it. And the main thing is that she would be here with you.”

“I just . . . I don’t know. I guess I found myself falling for this girl I just met. Maybe it was meant to be just an amazing fling, not something long term.”

Everyone was quiet for a moment. Katrina thought about Willow. She wondered what she was doing in that moment. Katrina wanted to call her but she hesitated. Maybe there was something to the way Saura broke up with her. Maybe the best thing is just to let go.

Devon pulled up to Katrina's house. The two walked into the dark house. Katrina turned her lights on. Suddenly she was back into her reality: she was home and there was no Saura and no Willow.

"Take a breather, and get your ass to the restaurant. I can't wait to show you all that I have done." Devon smiled.

The friends hugged before Devon walked out. Katrina locked the door behind her. She pulled her large suitcase into her bedroom and threw it on the bed. She opened it to find a box sitting on top of her clothes. She sat on the side of the bed and opened the box. Inside was a digital picture frame. She turned it on to see photos of her and Willow's experiences flashing on the screen. She smiled; she didn't know when Willow had time to make it, but it was the best souvenir she had.

Katrina opened her computer and clicked on the Skype application. She pressed talk on Willow's name.

Willow almost jumped out of her skin when she heard her Skype ringing from her phone. She jumped up and down when she saw Katrina's face appearing on the screen. Willow calmed herself down before she pressed talk.

"Hey, you," Willow casually responded.

"When did you have time to make this frame, sneaky woman?" Katrina smiled. She realized she was super excited to see Willow's face.

"When you were sleeping one night. Do you like it?"

"I love it," Katrina said as she admired the frame.

All her reason went out the window as she stared at Willow's beautiful face.

"Hey I'm opening my restaurant in two weeks. I want you to come to Memphis and be here when it opens."

"Are you sure? I know that is a really big night for you," Willow said trying to keep her cool.

Katrina knew it was crazy but she didn't care. There was something special growing between her and Willow and she wanted to explore it further. If Willow was willing to come to Memphis, why not have her there?

"So do you want to come?"

Willow pressed her lips together tightly. She rubbed her fingers against her chin. "I don't know. Are you willing to take me to Graceland?"

"Good Lord." Katrina rolled her eyes. She had lived in Memphis her whole life and never had a desire to go to Elvis's home. "Yes, I will take you to Graceland."

"Well in that case let me look at tickets." Willow blew Katrina a kiss before they hung up from each other.

Katrina and Willow both couldn't wait until they were in each other's arms again.

Katrina was still floating on cloud nine when she arrived at her restaurant. Her mouth dropped when she saw the new signs on the front of the building. Devon was waiting for her at the door. Katrina pulled in the spot with a sign saying RESERVED FOR KATRINA LIVINGSTON.

"Dee, I am already in love," Katrina said as she got out of her car.

Katrina walked to the door. She couldn't help but notice how quickly Devon had changed clothes. She traded the yoga pants and tank she picked her up in for a pair of pinstriped pants and a button-down shirt. Both outfits hugged her athletically toned body perfectly. Katrina knew Devon hadn't worked out that day as her hair was freshly flat ironed, something that she didn't do too often anymore since making the transition to being natural.

"Well wait 'til you see the inside." Devon smiled as she unlocked the front door.

The two walked in the building. Devon turned on the lights and watched as Katrina's mouth dropped open. The last time Katrina was in the building they were still fixing the structure; now the place was completely decked out. Devon began pointing out various design elements.

"So we decided that the concrete floors were rather perfect so we stained them instead of covering it with hardwood. So you have this deep brown texture but wait until the lights hit it at night, gorgeous."

Katrina didn't know if she was more in awe of the restaurant or Devon's eye for detail. It was much more than she ever expected. The large space was open and spacious but had an intimate feel with the large panel booth seating. The tables were the perfect color of blue giving a bit of color to the mostly earth-toned building. The main focus was the large aquarium filled with blue water and exotic fish. In the front was a stage with all the equipment needed for any band to have a great set.

"Devon, I fucking love it. Everything is more than I ever expected. How did you get all of this in budget?"

"I have my ways." Devon smiled. "You know, called in a few favors here and there; seems many places were very interested in being involved with the new up-and-coming restaurant."

Katrina wrapped her arms around Devon. She hugged her friend who had gone over and above for her. Devon excelled at anything she put her mind to.

"You really should do this shit full time; it's amazing." Katrina continued to admire her building.

"Maybe. I really enjoyed helping. Oh I hired an amazing manager to get the staff together. You are going to love him. So awesomely gay but he really knows his shit. Not to mention he can dress his ass off."

"Cool. So let me see my kitchen."

The women walked into the large kitchen. Katrina felt tears forming as she stood in the state-of-the-art kitchen. The most important part to her was the kitchen, and it was more than she ever expected.

"I have one surprise for you." Devon was smiling from ear to ear. She walked over to a wall that had a large sheet covering it. "I know the one thing you always wanted was a place to make your perfect pizzas. Well this was my special gift to you."

Devon pulled the sheet down. In the middle of the wall was a custom-made wood burning brick oven. Katrina's eyes swelled with tears. She turned around and wiped her eyes.

"Tree, don't cry." Devon ran up to her friend who was unable to speak at the moment.

Katrina couldn't control her emotions. Everything was better than she expected. As happy as she was, she couldn't help but feel fearful. Feeling as if she was going to faint, she took a seat on a stool in the kitchen.

"Devon, I am blown away. Everything is just . . . I don't know how to repay you."

Devon smiled. She loved helping her friends and Katrina was the best friend she had.

Katrina's face dropped. "Dee, what if I can't make this work? All this hard work goes down the drain—"

"No, Tree, you aren't allowed to think like that. Don't worry about any of this stuff. All you worry about is making excellent food. You could have none of the things outside, but if the food is good people will come. And your food is superb."

The friends hugged. Everything was coming together. After all the years of school and being a chef for other upscale restaurants now Katrina was the head of her own place. Devon showed Katrina how to turn everything off and set the alarm system for the restaurant before leaving.

"So I invited Willow to come here for the opening," Katrina said as she locked the door to the restaurant.

"That's cool. I probably should try to find a date somewhere." Devon frowned. The idea of dating was exhausting for her. She openly identified as bisexual, which was her downfall. Lesbians didn't want to date her because they didn't like the idea of coming after a man. Men wanted to date her in hopes of a threesome happening at some point. This caused the breakup with her most recent ex, Thomas, who just couldn't handle her having two lesbians as best friends.

"Willow has this friend named Piper; she is crazy but a super hot white girl. She kind of makes me think of Serena from *Gossip Girl.*" Katrina looked at Devon whose look of disapproval said it all.

"Last thing I need is crazy."

There was a silence between them. Katrina unlocked her door and turned back around to see Devon staring at her with a worried expression on her face.

"Dee, what is it?"

Devon stared at the ground while she fidgeted with her fingers.

"Devon?"

"Shanice called me." Devon turned her face but could still see the disapproval etched across Katrina's face.

"Dee."

"I haven't done anything. I just said that she called."

"How many times has she called? And the better question is how many times have you answered?"

Devon didn't want to answer the question. If there was one person she needed to stay away from, it was her ex-girlfriend Shanice. Katrina wanted to strangle her best friend. Shanice was like a drug to Devon. She was the first girl she ever slept with back in high school. She then proceeded to walk in and out of Devon's life whenever something better came along. Time would pass and when she felt like it was time to come back, Shanice would pop back up and Devon would always take her back. They had gone through the same thing from senior year until

Devon's final years in grad school. The final breakup was three years ago, when Shanice left Devon completely broken. Since then Devon hadn't seriously dated a single person, only Thomas, which Teri and Katrina both knew never was going to last.

"We talked once, maybe twice. She wanted to apologize for—"

"Whoa, let me guess, she wanted to apologize for breaking your heart again. And now she's in a much better place. What is she doing now? Is she deep into a new church or has she become Buddhist?" Katrina scowled.

"She meditates."

Katrina threw her hands in the air and let out a loud sigh.

"I am not going back, Tree. I just wanted to let you know."

"Devon, please, for the love of all things do not go back to that girl. She isn't worth it. Never has been. You know you deserve so much better." Katrina held her friend's hand.

"I know." Devon lowered her head.

"Good, now block that ass and let's find you someone else. There is someone perfect out there, I know it."

"Easy for you to say, you have had an amazing relationship and hell you go overseas and meet another freaking perfect woman. Stop taking all the women, Tree!" Devon pushed her friend.

"Maybe that's the problem, we have exhausted all possibilities in Memphis. Maybe you should do your *Eat, Pray, Love* thang somewhere."

"I have always wanted me an Australian." Devon smiled.

Devon and Katrina hugged again before getting in their separate cars. Katrina thought about what Devon said. Her relationship with Saura was amazing but she couldn't help but hold resentment for the way she left her. Then she met Willow, which was blowing her mind all over again. Neither Teri nor Devon had had meaningful relationships in years. Teri was happy living like a bachelor where Devon craved love, but the right one hadn't come along. Katrina never cared if she had love, but somehow she found two. She only could pray her friends experienced the feelings she had sometime soon.

Katrina was happy to open the door to her house. In the darkness she noticed the red light flashing on her cordless phone. She didn't think to check her home phone voicemail while she was gone because everyone of any importance knew to call her cell phone. She pressed the voicemail button, which alerted her of two missed messages.

"Hey, um, hi, Tree. I know you are probably in Europe right now. I didn't want to bother you on your trip. I just wanted to let you know that I was thinking of you."

Saura's voice was haunting. Katrina held the phone as the machine's voice asked if she wanted to delete the message. Katrina's body was frozen; she didn't know what to push. As the female's voice repeated the various options Katrina pressed seven to save the message. The next message began to play.

"Hey, Katrina, it's me again. I'm sure you are wondering why I am calling again. I just . . . Well things aren't as perfect as I imagined. I can almost hear you telling me that things aren't always going to be perfect. I guess that's why I'm calling. As much as I want to talk to you, I know I don't need to. I just wanted to hear your voice. Anyway, I'll go now. I hope your trip is everything you expected it to be."

Katrina hadn't heard Saura sound so sad before. She pressed the caller ID to see if there was a phone number, but all she saw was a bunch of unknown number messages. Panic set in; she wondered if Saura was all right.

Katrina ran to her bedroom and unpacked her carryon backpack. She grabbed her iPad and pulled up Facebook. She typed in Saura's name. Saura had a new profile photo. It was obviously a professional photo in black and white that was absolutely stunning. Katrina stared at the photo that made Saura look like an old Hollywood starlet. Katrina began to scroll through her profile. She saw photos of what had to be the house she was living in and some of the women she was with.

Katrina noticed a familiar face in all the photos. A stud with a short Mohawk seemed to be very close to Saura in all of the photos. Even in group photos the stud was always near Saura, usually with her arm on her in some kind of way. Katrina got an uneasy feeling. Most of the photos seemed to have one person liking them. She clicked on the name, which took her to the stud's profile.

Katrina's blood began to boil. Her photos weren't nearly as innocent as Saura's. In photos she saw Saura hugging the stud. The girl had captions on photos calling Saura the bae, or boo. She scrolled through her timeline until one status caught her attention:

Picking bae up from the airport, so happy she is finally here.

Katrina noticed the time stamp. It was the day that Saura left.

Katrina's hands were trembling. She wanted to stop herself but she couldn't. She looked at more photos until one slapped her in her face. A photo of Saura kissing the stud, dated just days after she made it to Los Angeles, covered Katrina's iPad screen. Katrina dropped the iPad on the bed. Her eyes lost focus, as the images played over and over in her mind. Saura not only left, but had lined up a new chick to take her place. The missing puzzle pieces were suddenly coming in to place. Saura left because she didn't want Katrina to consider coming to L.A.

Everything was red. She wanted to fly to Los Angeles just to slap the shit out of Saura. Suddenly Katrina was questioning everything. How long did she know the girl? Had she been cheating on her the whole time? Katrina jumped up off her bed and ran to the living room. She didn't want anything reminding her of the dirty bitch. She grabbed a Rubbermaid container and began pulling all the photos off the wall and bookshelves. She pulled the comforter set off the bed along with the sheets and curtains that Saura had picked out. Saura had small traces of her Asian heritage throughout the house. Katrina went through grabbing Buddha statues and Asian portraits, throwing them in the box until it was too heavy to hold anymore.

Katrina went to grab her keys to take the trash out when she heard a faint beeping. She walked in her room to see her iPad was making the noise. She pressed the button and noticed that she had missed a call from Willow on Skype and had a voicemail. She pressed the play and Willow's face appeared on the screen with Piper in the background.

"Hey you, I know you are probably out with your friends," Willow said in her bubbly voice. Piper was waving and making funny faces in the background. "I just wanted to let you know that I was thinking about you. Piper says hi. Okay, talk to you later," Willow blew a kiss before the message closed.

Katrina fell to her bed. The red she was seeing quickly turned back to regular colors. Emotions flooded through her. The pain she never truly allowed herself to feel was trying to break through the wall she had carefully built up. Even with someone as amazing as Willow wanting to be with her, she realized she didn't have time to heal from Saura. She noticed the room she had destroyed in less than five minutes. If Saura had that type of effect on her she knew that she wasn't over her.

Katrina started regretting her decision. Was it right to have Willow in America if she was still in love with another woman? She wanted to call her back and tell her that it wasn't a good idea but something stopped her. If Saura can be with someone else why should she ruin a good thing because of her? Katrina shook her head.

"Fuck you, Saura!" Katrina yelled at the top of her lungs. She wasn't going to let her feelings for Saura ruin anything she could have with Willow or anyone else. It was obvious that Saura never deserved her love to begin with.

Katrina took all of Saura's leftovers out and threw them away. She grabbed some of her old sheets and put them on the bed. Her first night home and the bed actually felt like it used to, before someone occupied the other half. Katrina knew one thing: the way to get over one is to get under another. Suddenly she couldn't wait for Willow's arrival.

Chapter 11

The doorbell woke Devon out of her sleep. She slowly made her way through her house, squinting her eyes at the sunlight coming in through her windows. She opened the door to find an Edible Arrangements delivery person standing there.

"I am looking for Devon Livingston," the delivery person said staring at the note on the arrangement.

"That is me. What is this?" Devon said as she signed the clipboard.

The delivery person handed the large box to her and quickly walked away. Devon stared at the box as she closed the door. She set the heavy package on the bar and pulled the card off of the package.

Just to say sorry again.

There was no name on the card, but she didn't need a name to know who it was from. Devon opened the box to find a lavish spread of strawberries and pineapples, her two favorite fruits. Some of the fruit was dipped in white and dark chocolate where the majority was left normal. The pineapples were cut in various shapes from hearts to daisies while the strawberries were on cabob sticks in between pineapple balls.

Devon knew she shouldn't but she couldn't resist. She took a bite out of one of the pineapple stars. The juice ran down the side of her mouth. She wiped the pineapple juice off her chin and licked her finger. There was one thing she knew: Shanice still knew the things to make her smile.

Devon grabbed her phone as she munched on another pineapple star. She scrolled in her caller ID until she saw her ex's name. The phone rang twice before Shanice picked up.

"Pineapples and strawberries huh?" Devon said smacking in the phone.

"Well I had to do something to get your attention." Shanice's smooth voice gave Devon chills.

"It was very nice, but help me understand why you feel the need to get my attention?"

There was a brief pause. "Maybe I am trying to make up for my bad behavior."

Devon held the phone. She knew this act very well. Shanice, also coming from a very wealthy family, had no problem showering Devon with expensive gifts. Devon was always left with those gifts to haunt her whenever Shanice broke her heart again. Katrina's voice rang through her head. She was right; Shanice was doing the exact same thing that she always did.

"Look, Shanice, as nice as the arrangement is, please do not think that you are going to be able to throw a few gifts my way and magically appear back in my life. This is not that anymore."

"Devon, trust me, I know there is no need to come to you the way I might have done in the past. We are thirty now. I know that I can't come at you with some twenty-year-old bullshit."

"Has it crossed your mind that you can't come to me at all anymore?" Devon sat on her sofa. Memories of sitting on that same couch, crying her eyes out the last time Shanice left, were locked in her brain. Shanice was her drug; she had to stay clean this time.

"Dev, I am not trying to date you again. I know that ship has sailed. Honestly I just really miss the friendship we had. No matter all the mess you were always one of my closest friends. I trust you more than I've ever trusted anyone. It's part of the reason I always came back to you."

Shanice's low, smoky voice always turned Devon on. She knew how to speak just to make Devon's body respond.

"Well." Devon's voice quavered. "You should have probably thought about that before you left me for, oh what's her name again? Peaches, Apple, Plum?"

"It was Hershey," Shanice replied.

"Oh that's right, the dumbest name in history."

There was another brief silence between them. Devon felt her body betraying her. She had a mix of anger, hurt, and arousal. Shanice was the only person who could make her mad and turn her on at the same time.

"Devon, I don't want to hurt you anymore. I know I'm asking for a lot but I don't want us to be like this with each other. I just hope one day we can work on friendship, or at least be acquaintances."

Devon was at a loss of words. She remembered the good times they had. Shanice made her laugh just as much as she made her cry. Devon didn't know if with their history if any kind of relationship could be possible.

"I have to go, Shanice. Thank you for the fruit."

Devon paused while waiting on a response from Shanice. She could hear her breathing on the line, but she wouldn't say anything.

"Shanice? Did you hear me?"

"Yeah," her voice finally echoed through the speaker. "If you need anything, Devon, know that I am always here. No matter what."

A smile crept up on Devon's face. She hung the phone up feeling a sense of accomplishment. She didn't let Shanice back in, and from the way she sounded she knew Shanice knew it wasn't going to be the way things used to be.

Chapter 12

The days seemed to be going by so slowly. Willow was anxious about her trip. Not only was she going to a country she had never been to, but she would be with the woman she couldn't stop thinking about.

She spent her days creating dresses just for her trip. She wanted to look special for Katrina. She played around with different prints she got from the fashion district in London. Piper gushed over the garments always finding a way to try them on.

Willow and Katrina couldn't talk as much as she wanted due to Katrina's busy schedule. She was creating dishes and training her kitchen so that it would run as efficiently as possible on opening day. There was going to be a huge pre-opening party where press and special guests were able to try the food before the actual opening. Willow designed a flowing dress that was perfect with a beautiful charcoal fabric with a blue abstract print on the bottom of it. Willow fit the dress perfectly to her body. She knew she would stand out in the creation.

Willow spent her free time researching Memphis and surrounding areas. The only thing she knew about the city was it was where Elvis was from. She remembered there being a big stir when the royal princes attended a wedding there once, but besides that she was clueless. She watched movies based in Memphis on Redbox. Katrina got a kick out of her watching *Hustle & Flow* for the first time.

Willow made lists of all the things she wanted to experience with Katrina. She wanted to ride the River Queen and get drunk on Beale Street. She wanted to check out the zoo and go to local lesbian clubs, even though Katrina said she didn't even go to the lesbian and gay clubs in the city.

Katrina seemed more interested in showing her other parts of the South. She talked about going to New Orleans and Atlanta, and seeing an arch in St. Louis. Willow knew in the end there was only one place she was craving to see, and that was Katrina's house, particularly her bed. If she never saw a piece of the city she would be okay with it as long as she was lying next to Katrina.

"So yeah, I need a dress to wear out with Corrie tonight; can I borrow one of these?" Piper walked in the room holding two of the short skater dresses Willow had created.

"No," Willow said as she pinned the hem of her newest creation.

"Oh come on, what is the purpose of me having a fashion designer friend if she never lets me wear any of the fashions? Come on, Willow, use me as your personal business card. These legs should be in this dress."

Piper held up the red skater dress. She poked her bottom lip out and batted her fake eyelashes.

"Oh okay, fine, but get one thing on that dress and I'm going to kill you."

Piper squealed her normal high-pitched squeal as she ran out of the room. Willow continued to hem until Piper appeared in the doorway completely transformed. She put on a pair of high-heeled boots with the short dress. She had to admit Piper made her clothes look amazing.

"Well I'm off. Ta-ta, friend."

Piper pranced out of the door as Willow's computer began to ring the familiar Skype sound. She sat down at the table, ran her hand through her hair quickly and pressed answer. Katrina's face appeared; she was sitting in her office wearing her white chef's jacket.

"Hey you." Willow smiled.

"Hey, I am so sorry I've been running around like a madwoman these last few days."

"No need, I totally understand." Willow shook her head when she noticed her hair was looking kind of funny.

"You look beautiful as usual." Katrina knew whenever Willow shook her head in the camera it was because she didn't like her hair.

"Yeah, right. How are things coming along?"

Katrina began explaining the changes to the menu she made. She added some new pasta dishes that were similar to things they tried while in Italy. Willow could listen to her talk about food all day. She loved how excited Katrina got over food and wine.

"So while I have you on the phone let me write down what time your flight gets in," Katrina said grabbing a pen.

"Saturday, noon."

"Okay, I will be at the airport to pick you up."

"Hey I know that day is going to be crazy for you. I can just take a cab to the hotel."

"Hotel? What hotel?" Katrina's confused face amused Willow.

"I thought it might be best that I stay at a hotel for the first few days."

"Why?"

"I know you are busy I don't want to be in the way."

"Babe, you not being in my bed is going to be a problem." Katrina stared directly into the camera. She wanted Willow to see how serious she was.

A loud noise came from the kitchen startling both of them.

"Okay let me go cancel that room immediately."

Katrina blew a kiss at Willow. Willow hung up with the same floating feeling she got whenever she talked to Katrina.

Willow stood in her dress after finishing the alterations. She studied her curves to make sure everything was lying in the right place. She paused when her cell phone started ringing. Willow picked up her phone to see an unknown number flashing. She thought about not answering but something told her to pick it up.

"Hello?"

"Willow, it's Corrie," Corrie said in a panic.

Willow heard a lot of racket coming from the other end of the phone. "Corrie, what is going on?"

"I need you to come get your friend; she's going crazy."

Willow grabbed her keys and ran out of the house. She got in her car driving as quickly as she could toward Corrie's house. Luckily Corrie didn't live too far, but even with a bit of London traffic it could cause a delay. Corrie lived in an urban part of the city surrounded by pubs and nightclubs. Seeing people, tons of people, out in the streets was a normal thing. Willow pulled up noticing a group of people standing around Corrie's home.

"Fucking bastard!"

Willow ran up to see Piper being held back by two men who seemed to be enjoying the moment most of all.

"Whoa what is going on?" Willow yelled as she ran to her friend.

"What's going on is I found this fucktard sleeping with that twat!" Piper's words spit out like venom.

"Who you calling a twat you fucking slut!" The unattractive girl attempted to charge toward Piper but was stopped by Corrie and two other men.

"The fuck, Corrie?" Willow cursed.

"The hell, Willow, I told your friend it was over but she is mental as usual."

"Mental? I'll show you mental!" Piper attempted to break through but the men held her tight.

Willow stood in front of Piper. She put her hands on her friend's shoulders in an effort to calm her down. "Piper, come with me, she's not worth it. Neither one of them are."

"Get her out of here before someone calls the bobbies," Corrie yelled.

Willow rolled her eyes at Corrie before turning back to her furious friend. "Let's get out of here before the police show up. Come with me, friend."

Piper froze when she heard a siren. She grabbed her purse off the ground and took Willow by her hand. "Don't ever bloody call me again!"

"I won't!" Corrie yelled as Willow closed the door behind Piper.

"Sod off, Corrie, you piece of shit. Stay away from my friend!" Willow got in her car and quickly drove off.

Piper started crying as soon as she got in the car. Willow rubbed her friend's hair while trying to pay attention to the traffic.

"I am such an idiot," Piper cried.

"No, you aren't. She is for treating you this way," Willow said as she waited at a light.

She knew as a friend she had to say that, but deep down she did feel Piper was crazy for continuing to deal with Corrie. She could only hope this time would be the final time. Piper's high voice pierced Willow's ears as she continued to wail.

Once calm, Piper explained that she had a fight with Corrie and was going to her home in an attempt to make up. It wasn't farfetched considering it was what they did all the time. Still having a key to Corrie's home, she let herself in only to find Corrie with her face buried between the woman's legs.

"I am done this time. I never want to see her again." Piper's voice cracked.

"Good, honey, let's go inside. I'll make you some tea."

Willow arrived at her flat and helped Piper inside. Before the tea kettle could whistle Piper was knocked out on her sofa. She covered her friend up with a blanket before retiring to her room. Willow crawled in to her bed. She couldn't stop thinking about Katrina. A familiar insecurity entered her mind. The reason she never dated seriously was because she never wanted to be in the situation Piper was in. She pushed those thoughts to the back of her head. Katrina was different; she knew it in her heart. Willow knew Katrina was the one; she only hoped Katrina truly felt the same way. In three days she would know for sure.

Chapter 13

Willow couldn't get off the plane quick enough. Her master plan was coming together perfectly. She grabbed her carryon bag and rushed off the plane as soon as she could. The Memphis airport was very different from what she was used to, but the airport was the least of her concerns. She was happy she didn't have to go through customs again. She endured that disaster at the Chicago airport. She filled out the customs forms and answered the rude agent's dumb questions before they let her through the gate. The flight to Memphis was packed; she was glad she upgraded to business class, even if it was for the shorter flight.

Willow arrived in the baggage claim area of the Memphis airport. She saw a girl with natural hair in a twist out standing near the belt, holding an iPad with her name across it. She smiled, recognizing Devon's face from pictures she'd seen.

Devon had seen plenty of photos of Willow but never imagined she would be even better looking in person. She definitely had her own style about her. Willow's curls bounced as she skipped toward Devon.

"Finally," Devon said as she held her arms out.

"Devon, pleasure to finally meet you, darling." Willow hugged Devon.

"Oh listen to that accent, too cute."

The buzzer rang as the bags started falling to the luggage belt.

"So how was the flight?" Devon asked as she sized up Willow. The beauty was obvious but very different from Saura. Where Willow had a more down-to-earth appeal, Saura had a much more exotic look to her. Willow looked like the girl you take home, where Saura was the girl you took to an awards show.

"Bloody long, but that doesn't matter. I'm here now. Does she know anything?"

Devon shook her head. She received a call from Willow a week before letting her know the plan. Willow was going to tell Katrina that her flight was delayed until the next day, which would mean she missed the party. Devon was to pick her up at the airport and take her to a hotel where she would catch a cab and surprise Katrina at the party. Everything was working out perfectly. Katrina was upset she was missing the party, but was too busy to think that anything was up.

"So the hotel I got you isn't far from the restaurant. I checked you into the Madison, which is one of the nicest hotels in the city," Devon said as Willow grabbed her bag.

"Thank you so much, Devon." Willow smiled.

"No problem, anything to make Katrina happy."

The two headed out of the airport to Devon's car. Memphis at first glance didn't leave anything for Willow to be excited about. As soon as they hit downtown her feeling changed. It was very different from London, but had an exciting feel about it. She noticed immediately how courteous everyone seemed to be.

Devon dropped Willow at the front door of the hotel. She had to get back to the restaurant to make sure everything was going according to plan. Willow was shocked at how spacious the room was. Standard hotel rooms in London were usually very small; sometimes the two beds would actually touch one another in a twin room. She had a large king-sized bedroom and a bathroom the size of her bedroom in her flat.

Willow couldn't resist the urge to run and jump on the plush bed. She closed her eyes. In a few short hours she would be back in Katrina's arms.

Teri rushed to finish the paperwork for her office. She knew Katrina would kill her if she was late for the opening. Ming stood in the doorway to Teri's office.

"What do you think?" Ming asked holding up a light pink shirt.

"I think it's very pink," Teri said only glancing at the shirt for a quick second.

"I know right. I am going to be the belle of the ball tonight, honey, just you wait and see." Ming threw his hair as if he had a head full of hair. Teri couldn't help but laugh when Ming let the flaming side of him show.

"Party tonight?"

The voice caused the both to turn their heads. Standing in the pharmacy was Vivian. Teri resisted the urge to stare at her chocolate legs in the short skirt she had on. Teri could almost picture her completely naked, wearing just her doctor's jacket she had on.

"Um, something like that," Teri sat up in her chair. She felt nervous all of a sudden.

"Don't be modest, Teri. Her best friend is opening a restaurant tonight." Ming's voice completely changed. He was back in professional mode sounding like the average Asian man.

"Oh that sounds exciting. I'm sure it will be amazing. I just came down to say hello to you. It's been awhile. I guess you were right about being locked back here." Victoria giggled.

"Oh well looks like you have the key to the lock, so never be a stranger." Teri smiled.

Victoria's eyes locked on Teri. They stared at each other as if to see who would buckle first. Ming watched the stare down going on. He remembered what his boyfriend said. There did seem to be an attraction there.

"Oh, Ms. Gold—"

"Call me Victoria," she said without taking her eyes off Teri.

"Well, Victoria, you should come tonight. It's going to be a very nice event." Ming nodded his head.

"I'm sure there's like a list or something," Victoria shook her head.

"Hello, it's Teri's best friend. She can get you on the list." Ming suddenly didn't care about his demeanor. It was obvious to him that he was in the presence of family. "Isn't that right, Teri?"

Teri couldn't take her eyes off Victoria. She could see herself fucking Victoria right on her desk. Ming hitting her desk was the only thing to bring her back to reality.

"Oh, yeah, I can put you as my plus one if you would like to come."

Victoria's right side of her mouth curled up. She focused back on Teri. "That actually sounds great. It's a date then?"

"Yeah. A date," Teri replied.

Teri and Ming watched as Victoria sashayed out of their office. As soon as the door closed Ming's head flung back around toward Teri.

"You little sneaky bitch." Ming sat in the chair next to Teri's desk.

"What are you talking about?" Teri said glancing back down at the paperwork on her desk.

"You and Victoria, why didn't you tell me?"

"Because there wasn't anything to tell. I'm just as shocked right now as you are."

Ming crossed his legs. He picked up a piece of paper and started fanning himself. "Whatever; all I know is it is hot in here and I bet it going to be an inferno in the party tonight."

Teri shook her head as Ming left for the night. She sat in her chair thinking about the encounter. Victoria was going to be her date for the night. Teri decided the paperwork could wait. She no longer could wear something out of her closet; she needed a new outfit for the night.

Chapter 14

Katrina watched as the crowd started to swell outside the restaurant. She was a wreck. Her hands were clammy and her heart felt like it was going to beat right out of her chest. She watched as press snapped photos of local dignitaries as they arrived. She couldn't believe some of the faces that were walking in the door.

Devon knocked on the door two times before walking in. She knew she looked amazing in her black pencil dress that was fitting the curves she worked hard to achieve. Her hair was laid; the Brazilian blowout was worth every penny she spent for it.

"Hey, Chef, it's almost time for your big debut." Devon smiled.

Her smile quickly changed when she saw the terrified expression on Katrina's face. Devon ran as quickly as her heels would allow her toward her friend who was mid panic attack.

"Calm down Katrina. Misty!"

A short girl wearing black pants and a black button-down appeared in the door.

"Water!" Devon fanned Katrina as the girl ran to get water.

"I don't know what is happening to me. I can't do this." Katrina fought to catch her breath.

"It's just a little panic attack, take deep breaths."

"What's up, bitches! Oh shit what is happening?" Teri said as she ran over to her friends.

"She's just having a little panic attack, right?" Devon stared at Teri who quickly caught the message she was trying to send.

"Oh yeah, just a little panic attack. Calm down, Tree; it's going to be okay." Teri ran out of the room as Misty arrived with water.

Katrina tried to sip the water but it wasn't helping. She was freaking completely out. Her chef's jacket felt like it was strangling her. She pulled at the jacket until all the clasps unsnapped. She pulled the jacket off and threw it on the ground.

"Tree, please calm down." Devon continued to fan her friend.

"What the fuck was I thinking? This is a horrible idea." Katrina shook her head feverishly. "I can't do this."

"Fuck outta here with that, dude." Teri appeared back in the door holding a bottle of Patrón. She put three shot glasses on the table, and opened the brand new bottle. She poured three shots into the shot glasses and handed one to each of her friends.

"You can do this. You were born to do this. Now suck that shit up and take the shot."

Teri held her glass up. Katrina looked at Devon who followed holding her glass close to Teri's. Katrina's body started to cool off. She continued to take deep breaths as she held the glass up to her friends.

"This is to the best fucking chef in all of Memphis; hell in all of the fucking South!"

The friends clicked the glasses against each other and swallowed the shots. The tequila burned, but lit a fire in Katrina that she needed. She picked up her jacket.

"Let's do this."

The building was packed. The live band played covers of R&B classics as waiters walked around with trays of small sample portions of the restaurant's signature dishes. Devon charmed reporters making sure they knew what to say in their publications the next day. Katrina made sure the kitchen was running perfectly before going back in her office to change into her suit for the night.

Carlos and Ming walked up to Teri who was nursing a drink at the bar. Carlos looked like something straight out of *GQ* magazine. Ming was dressed to impress in his black suit with pink shirt and pink and black bowtie. Teri laughed at the women who were quickly disappointed when they realized Carlos was there with Ming.

"This is fabulous, honey; your girl did her thang," Carlos said as he shook Teri's hand.

"It is amazing isn't it?" Teri said. She had to admit she was proud of her friend.

"So where is your date?" Ming batted his eyes.

"Oh yes, Ming told me about sexual chocolate coming to see you today."

Both men nudged each other playfully. Teri shrugged her shoulders. Victoria hadn't made it and she was starting to think she was being stood up.

"Hey let me get you guys a drink on me." Teri smiled.

"Bitch, the drinks are free." Ming playfully hit Teri. The three toasted to the special occasion.

"Oh . . . my . . . Gawd." Ming's face dropped.

Teri and Carlos both turned around. Walking toward them was Victoria. Her hair was pulled back in a perfect bun. Teri felt the heat rising as she studied the tight red dress Victoria was sporting. The diamond bracelet caught the light causing a flash of light to sparkle in Teri's eyes.

"Hi, guys," Victoria greeted the group.

"Okay, don't sue me, because, honey, I am not coming on to you, but damn you are wearing that dress." Carlos took Victoria by her hand, spinning her around. Victoria hugged Carlos giving Teri time to check out her ass. Teri could practically picture her bent over.

Victoria turned to Teri. She flashed her white smile.

"Thank you for the invitation, this is quite the gathering," Victoria said admiring the décor.

"Not a problem, anytime." Teri wrapped her arms around Victoria. Her aroma only heightened Teri's attraction. "Would you like a drink?"

"Are you going to try to get me liquored up?" Victoria smirked.

"Do you want me to get you liquored up?" Teri threw professional out the window. She wanted this woman.

"It doesn't really matter." Victoria leaned in toward Teri's ear. "I plan on fucking you regardless."

The statement caught Teri off guard. She watched as Victoria held her hand up to get the bartender's attention.

Devon was in her element as she chatted with the mayor and his wife. She wanted to pat herself on the back. She managed to get everyone out to the event. It was going to be talked about for weeks. She wanted to treat herself to a drink but decided to wait 'til later in the night.

Something caught her eye. She watched as Katrina walked out of the kitchen. Katrina wasn't in her kitchen wear anymore. She traded her chef's jacket for a pair of tailored pants, a shirt, and a vest. The bowtie finished off her look.

"This is amazing." Katrina wrapped her arms around Devon.

"Katrina, meet the mayor and his wife." Devon pulled away from Katrina; for some reason she didn't want to be so close to her.

Katrina shook hands with the mayor who congratulated her on the restaurant. Devon couldn't take her eyes off of Katrina. Suddenly she wasn't seeing her best friend anymore; it was something more. Devon noticed a familiar face standing at the front door. Before she could say anything another person began to tell her how amazing the place was.

"Amazing!" Teri said as she walked up with Victoria. "Guys, this is Victoria Gold; she is the new chief of staff at my hospital.

Devon and Katrina greeted Victoria. Both were shocked to see the gorgeous woman with Teri. Teri usually had horrible taste in women and always seemed to date ratchet women who were just so excited to date someone who didn't ride the bus.

"Holy shit is that your girl?" Teri said as she stared at a woman at the door.

"What?" Katrina turned around. Her face dropped. "Oh my God."

Devon watched as Katrina made her way through the crowd. Willow and Katrina both looked like kids in a candy store.

Katrina knew her eyes had to be deceiving her. Her heart pounded as she got closer and closer. Willow finally caught her eye and a huge smile covered her face. Katrina put her hands on Willow's shoulders.

"Is it really you?"

Willow nodded her head. Katrina looked even better than she imagined.

"What are you doing here?" Katrina couldn't figure out what to say. She stared at Willow as if it was the first time seeing her.

"I wanted to surprise you. Devon picked me up from the airport this morning. Are you surprised?"

"Am I." Katrina picked Willow up in her arms. The two hugged each other as if it had been years instead of a few weeks.

Katrina took Willow by her hand and led her through the crowd. She joined her friends at the bar. Katrina picked Devon up, squeezing her tight.

"I should kill you." Katrina kissed Devon on her cheek.

"Surprise!" Devon clapped her hands together.

"Hey, Teri, this is my Willow," Katrina said as she put her arm around Willow.

Willow shook Teri's and Victoria's hands as Devon motioned for the bartender.

"You guys, this night is better than anything I ever expected. And now it's perfect."

Katrina grabbed her drink and Willow's hand. She and Devon walked up on the stage as the band was finishing their rendition of "Let's Get it On." The singer handed Devon the microphone. Willow watched along with Teri as Devon introduced Katrina.

The crowd gave a rousing round of applause for Katrina as she bowed to the crowd.

"I just want to take a moment to thank everyone for coming out tonight. I know there are a million places you could be and I'm just glad you chose to be here with me tonight."

The crowd let out a loud round of applause. Katrina winked at Willow. Willow was so proud to be there with Katrina and her friends. Katrina held her hand out. Devon joined her in the middle of the stage.

"I also want to thank this incredible woman right here. Devon has been my eyes and ears and honestly this place would not be where it is without her. You are more than my best friend; you are my sister."

Katrina hugged Devon as the crowd clapped. She handed the mic back to the singer as the band began to perform their rendition of "Celebration" by Kool & the Gang. Katrina and Devon walked off the stage. They shook the hands of people as they made it to the floor. Katrina couldn't get back to Willow quick enough. The dress Willow was wearing was hanging off her curves, showing off her round butt and plump breasts. Katrina wrapped her arms around Willow. She kissed her on the nape of her neck as they danced to the music.

The dance floor was packed. The friends danced together. Devon danced with Carlos and Ming while Victoria ground her ass against Teri. Willow and Katrina were in their own world, slow dancing even when a fast song was playing.

"Have I told you how happy I am that you are here?" Katrina said after pecking Willow on her lips.

"Yes, but you can say it as much as you like."

A tap on Katrina's shoulder caused her to look away from Willow. Misty stood on the dance floor. "The mayor wants to get a photo with you before they leave and the sous chef needs to see you in the kitchen."

Katrina frowned. "Duty calls. Hey, Ming, will you dance with my girl until I get back?"

"Of course I will," Ming said as he twirled over to Willow.

Katrina said her good-byes to the mayor and smiled for pictures with him and members of the city council. She checked in with the kitchen to make sure everything was running correctly. Katrina was flying. She went into her office to catch her breath. The night was years in the making but finally all her hard work looked like it was paying off. She sat in her desk chair just to take a moment to absorb everything that was happening.

"Looks like the restaurant is a hit."

Katrina froze. She couldn't stop staring at the wall. She didn't want to turn around. She knew it couldn't be who she thought it was. Against better judgment she slowly turned around to her desk. It seemed like she was staring at a ghost.

There standing in the doorway of her office was Saura.

Chapter 15

"Congratulations, baby, you did it."

Saura took a few steps into the office. Katrina didn't believe she was standing there. She looked amazing as usual. She looked like she had just stepped off the cover of a magazine in the long turquoise dress that dipped low in the front and hugged her thighs.

"Saura, what are you doing here?"

Katrina didn't know what to make of the surprise. Saura closed the door behind her. She turned her head and her bouncy hair whipped around with her head.

"I couldn't miss your grand opening." Saura smiled. She didn't know what kind of reaction she was going to get but the silence wasn't expected.

Katrina didn't know what to make of the moment. Out of nowhere the image of the spiky hair stud she was kissing on Facebook entered her face. Anger began to set in. "You really shouldn't have."

"Tree, I know the way I left was difficult but I thought we were in a good space when we talked last."

"A good space." Katrina stood up. "Yeah, we were, until I went on Facebook and saw your little girlfriend."

Saura looked like a deer caught in headlights. "Katrina, wait a moment."

"No, you wait!" Katrina walked from behind her desk. "How fucking dare you come here like nothing is wrong when you were fucking cheating on me with that bitch!"

"I never cheated on you." Saura took a step back.

"Oh, so now I'm a fool too? You think I didn't see the time stamps. The girl saying how she was excited to have her boo in town. The fuck, Saura, was all we had a fucking joke? How long were you fucking off with her?"

"Katrina, I wasn't fucking off with her. She was my ex-girlfriend and yes, she did pick me up from the airport because we were friends. The pictures you saw were from when we were together back in Atlanta, not from Los Angeles. Didn't you notice that my hair was lighter?"

Katrina tried to remember her hair in the photo.

"Okay, so if that is the case why were they recently uploaded?"

"Because she was trying to win me back, Katrina, you have to believe me. I haven't messed with anyone while in Los Angeles. Hell, I couldn't stop thinking about you."

Katrina felt her guard breaking down. Saura looked even better than she did when she was in Memphis. Katrina couldn't help but wonder if she was telling the truth.

"Katrina, I am miserable. I miss you so much that I can barely concentrate out there. I live with a bunch of ditsy models who starve themselves and fuck random men all the time. I found myself calling the house phone over and over just to hear your voice."

Katrina remembered how many times she saw the unavailable message on her phone. Saura walked closer. She grabbed Katrina's hand.

"I know that I messed up. I don't know if you can forgive me. But, I love and miss you so much. I just want to be with you, in our home."

Katrina's heart was beating fast. She felt her pulse racing. She felt herself drawn to Saura. Her exotic beauty was pleading to come back home. She didn't realize how bad she missed her. Katrina felt the wall breaking completely down.

Willow's face entered her mind.

Katrina quickly pulled away from Saura. She felt overwhelming guilt coming over her. Standing in her office was the woman she thought she was going to be with forever, and outside, on the dance floor was the woman she saw a new future with.

"Tree, what the hell are you doing? Oh shit." Devon froze as the door opened and she saw Saura standing in front of Katrina. "Saura, what are you doing here?"

"I decided to come home. I missed Katrina too much. I had to come home."

"Welcome back." Devon hugged Saura while her eyes widened toward Katrina. Katrina shook her head and hands silently at Devon.

"It feels good to be back but, girl, you are squeezing me." Saura pulled away from Devon.

"Oh, sorry, girl. I'm just so surprised to see you, and as much as I hate to break this reunion up I need to talk to Katrina about some business stuff super quick. Can we have a moment? How about you go grab a drink from the bar?"

"Oh, okay." Saura was taken aback by the awkwardness of the two friends but she just shrugged her shoulders and walked out of the room.

Devon closed the door behind her. "What the fuck!" Devon threw her hands up.

"I have no idea. She just showed up," Katrina said trying to whisper in case Willow was outside the door.

Teri and Victoria were causing the temperature to rise on the dance floor. Victoria's soft ass ground against pelvis as Teri's hands held on to Victoria's thighs as she stood there taking all that Victoria was throwing at her.

"So was this your plan? Come here and try to turn me on?" Teri said in Victoria's ear.

"Well it was part of it." Victoria turned around wrapping her arms around Teri's neck. "I knew I wanted you the moment I stepped on the elevator."

"You know you could have just said something."

"I had to scope the scene first. That Carlos is one chatty man."

Teri looked at Carlos and Ming who were taking turns dancing with Willow. "Remind me to thank them later." Teri winked. "So got any plans after this?"

"I don't know," Victoria did a little dip as she slowly wound her body back up. "Do I?"

"You most certainly do."

A face appeared in the crowd causing Teri to pause. She stopped holding Victoria's thighs. Her mouth dropped open as she saw Saura standing at the bar.

"Holy shit!" Teri yelled causing Victoria to give her an inquisitive look. "Baby, give me one minute, I will be right back. Don't go anywhere."

Before Victoria could respond Teri disappeared into the crowd.

Devon paced the floor. Her perfect night had just taken a major turn for the worse. She didn't know what to do. Willow flew across the ocean to be with her and now Saura had flown across the States for the same thing.

"Dude, you won't believe who is outside." Teri came storming into the office.

By the looks on Devon and Katrina's faces she knew they already knew.

"What the fuck is she doing here?" Teri closed the door.

"She said she missed me and wanted to come back home."

"For good?" Teri folded her arms.

"Looks that way," Devon replied.

The three friends stared at each other in silence. Katrina was torn.

"Okay, so let's think about it like this. Saura left you to go to Los Angeles. You met someone else and you are moving on. That's her damn fault for leaving in the first place." Teri pointed at her friend.

"And, Katrina, Willow flew all this way to be with you. It would be wrong to leave her out in the cold," Devon added.

Katrina knew her friends were making sense but she couldn't deny the attraction that she felt the moment Saura walked into her office. She couldn't treat Willow wrong, she was amazing and she had deep feelings for her, but Katrina knew a piece of her heart still belonged to Saura.

"Saura and I have unfinished business. I can't just ignore that," Katrina said as she sat on the edge of her desk.

"But it's the past. Willow is out there hoping to be your future." Teri walked closer to her torn friend.

"But if Saura never left I never would have talked to Willow to begin with."

"It sounds to me like you are leaning more toward Saura." Devon folded her arms. "What are you going to do with Willow?"

"I am not leaning more to Saura, I am just . . . Fuck I don't know what I am doing. What am I going to do?"

"I say you tell Saura to kick rocks," Teri exclaimed. "She left you dog. No notice, no nothing. You didn't deserve that shit, just like Willow won't deserve you leaving her high and dry now."

Katrina knew Teri was right. Saura left her; why should she be given a second chance when she had someone wonderful already there for her? Katrina took a deep breath.

"Fuck this." Katrina poured herself a shot of Patrón and took it to the head. She headed out the door with her two friends following.

"You are just cute as can be," Ming said to Willow as he twirled her around.

"Thank you, so are you." Willow smiled. A face at the bar caught her eye. She knew that face very well. It was Katrina's ex. Willow's body tensed up. She took two steps forward just to make sure she was seeing who she thought. There was no denying it. When Katrina left she found herself looking at photos on Katrina's page. She saw the ex on a lot of them. She was gorgeous, even better looking than she remembered.

"What are we looking at?" Ming said standing next to Willow.

Suddenly Katrina appeared only steps away from the bar. She looked directly at Willow. Katrina rushed past Saura and toward Willow. Willow turned around but Katrina grabbed her arm.

"Willow—"

"Is that her? Is that Saura?"

Katrina's face lowered. She didn't know what she was supposed to say.

"Did you know she was going to be here?" Willow questioned trying to remain as calm as she could.

"No, I had no idea she was going to be here. I don't know what to say."

At the bar Saura watched the scene unfold with Katrina and the unfamiliar chick. She didn't know who the girl was or why Katrina passed her to go talk to her. Saura could tell from the look on the girl's face that she wasn't happy.

"Saura, funny seeing you here." Teri walked up with the bottle of Patrón in her hand.

"Hi, Teri. Who is that Katrina is talking to?"

Teri let out a laugh. "You see this funny thing happened when you left."

"Oh really, what was that?"

"Life kept moving on." Teri poured a shot in the glass Saura was holding. "Here, I think you are going to need this." Teri walked away laughing. She took Victoria by her hand and they walked out of the building.

Saura's face dropped. She knew that the girl was more than a friend.

Willow listened as Katrina told her that Saura surprised her. She didn't know what to think. She knew everything about the girl. She knew that they had only been broken up for a few weeks before she met Katrina. Katrina tried to assure her that she was there with her, but Willow couldn't help but have an uneasy feeling. In the end they were not together and Saura was the love of Katrina's life.

"We don't need to have this discussion here." Willow mustered up the strength to remain rational.

"Willow, I don't want you to be worried. Please don't be worried or upset," Katrina pleaded. She could almost feel Saura's eyes burning a hole in her back.

"I'm okay, really I am." Willow smiled. "You have things to do; don't be worried about me. I am a big girl."

"You are an amazing woman." Katrina hugged Willow. "I am going to finish up here and we can leave."

Willow smiled as she nodded her head. She forced herself not to look in the direction of Saura who she was sure was looking at them.

Katrina walked back toward her office. Saura quickly followed. The moment she made it back in the office she heard the door slam behind her.

"Who the fuck is that, Katrina?" Saura's voice raised an octave.

"Her name is Willow and I met her when I was in London."

"So you fucking meet some bitch in London and she comes back to Memphis. What the fuck, Katrina? Seriously? We hadn't been apart a month and you've already moved some bitch here?"

"You left me, Saura!" Katrina yelled. "Remember that? You left. And yes, I met someone who I really like while I was on the trip that we were supposed to take together."

"So you had a fling, you don't bring the bitch back with you!" Saura pushed Katrina.

"First off she's not a bitch, second off, you broke up with me!"

"So two years goes down the drain in a month. What does that say about our relationship?"

"It says that you fucking left me!" Katrina realized how loud she was. She took a deep breath to calm down.

Saura was pissed, but she knew in the end that she did leave Katrina. Saura put her hands on Katrina's arms. "Katrina, I am sorry I left, it was the worst decision of my life. But are you really willing to throw away all we have because of a mistake? I didn't cheat. I didn't sleep around. I am back and I want us to be back."

"It's not that easy, Saura."

"It can be. Tell me you don't still love me."

Katrina turned her head away. She knew she couldn't say the words.

"See it? You know you do."

Saura pulled Katrina's face toward hers. She planted her lips against Katrina's. Katrina couldn't fight it. She wrapped her arms around Saura as their tongues touched. Willow's face appeared in her head. Katrina pulled away.

"I can't do this. I can't do that to her. She's a nice girl."

"Yeah, but she isn't me." Saura took Katrina's hands and placed them on her ass. "Tell me you didn't miss all of this. 'Cause Lord knows I missed you."

The beast in Katrina was trying to come out. A knock on the door caused Katrina to jump back from Saura. She caught her breath as Devon opened the door.

"Guys, I don't know what is going on in here but I can tell you it's not the place for it. Katrina, you need to get out here and do your job," Devon said in her most professional voice.

"I dropped my things at our house. Was that a bad idea?" Saura smirked.

"It was a terrible idea," Katrina snapped.

"Well, since that's my only residence I guess I'll just go back there. See you when you get home."

Katrina's mouth dropped as Saura left the room. Devon closed the door behind her.

"She's at your house?"

Katrina shrugged her shoulders. She didn't know what to do or say.

"What are you going to do, Katrina?"

"Tonight I guess I'll be staying at the Madison with Willow. I'll figure out the rest tomorrow."

Willow sat at the bar nursing her drink. The crowd was almost gone. Ming and Carlos had gone and so had Teri and Victoria. Willow didn't know what to think about the night. She wondered what was happening in the back where Katrina disappeared with Saura. Thoughts were rushing through her mind until a finger tapped her on her shoulder. She turned around to find herself face to face with Saura.

"Hello, Willow, right? My name is Saura." Saura held her hand out.

"Hello," Willow said shaking Saura's hand.

"I just wanted to introduce myself. Looks like we are in a little pickle here."

Willow put her guard up. She didn't know why Saura was being so nice to her.

"Well I just wanted to come over here because I mean we are women; we can be adults about the situation. Katrina told me what happened and I totally get it."

Willow tilted her head. "I'm sorry, you totally get what?"

"Oh, nothing." Saura giggled. "Well I have to get out of here. Enjoy your night with her. I mean you totally deserve it for coming from all the way across the pond to see her. But just understand it will be the last one."

"Excuse me?" Willow felt her blood boiling.

"You heard me. Katrina might be a little confused right now. But it won't last. We are meant for each other. And no British bobble head is going to keep us apart. Have a good night."

Saura shot an evil smirk at Willow before walking away. Willow wanted to pull all of her hair out but refused to cause a scene in Katrina's establishment. Willow didn't know if she wanted to cry or fight. She watched as Katrina came out of the back with two of her staff members. Katrina looked at her and smiled as she walked up to her.

"So I have to close things down here but then we can leave."

"I think I'm going to go ahead and leave," Willow said trying to keep her composure.

Katrina was worried. She noticed the expression on Willow's face. "Are you sure? I mean, I really want to come with you."

Willow forced a smile. "No, baby, I mean I want to go before you. I will see you at the room; here is a key." Willow pulled an extra hotel key card out of her clutch.

"Okay, well I will be over there very soon. No more than an hour." Katrina kissed Willow on her forehead.

Willow arrived back at the room and instantly opened her iPad. She called Piper on Skype. In moments Piper's face covered the screen.

"What the fuck!" Piper screeched after Willow filled her in on the night.

"I don't know what to do, Piper. She is gorgeous, so fucking gorgeous."

"So are you." Piper sat back on her couch. "Fuck that bitch, she gave her up."

"I don't know what to do. Maybe I should just come home."

"No!" Piper jumped up holding her tablet in her hand. "Willow, you and Katrina are bloody perfect together. Don't let some twit come in and take what belongs to you now."

Willow nervously ran her hands through her hair. "I don't know what to do. I can't compete with someone she loved for years."

"Yes, you can. Obviously the girl wasn't all that if she was able to move on with you so fast. You just need to stake your claim."

"So, what do I do?"

Piper pointed at the screen. "You show her why she is with you. That girl might have the past, but remind Katrina that you can be her future. Shag her senseless and show her how we British girls do it."

Willow thought about what Piper was saying. She let Saura win the first battle but the war was far from over. She didn't come thousands of miles to go home without the woman she wanted. She was going to fight for what she wanted.

Chapter 16

Teri opened the door to her house. Victoria slipped out of her red bottoms and walked in the house as if she had been there a million times. Teri walked over to her wine shelf.

"Would you like something to drink?"

"Merlot if you have some."

Teri grabbed one of her more expensive bottles of wine. She knew that Victoria wasn't like the rest of the women she messed with who would be happy with some cheap moscato. This woman was different. She poured two glasses of wine, handing one to Victoria who was sprawled across her brown leather sofa.

"You have a nice place here," Victoria said as she took a sip of the merlot.

"Thank you, it's a work in progress." Teri took a sip too. "So, Ms. Gold, you said something to me earlier that I haven't been able to get out of my mind."

"Oh, you mean the part about fucking you? Yes, I have a tendency to be straight to the point."

"I see." Teri put her hand on Victoria's exposed thigh. "Well I usually don't sleep where I eat, ya feel me?"

Victoria nodded her head as Teri's hand made its way under her skirt. "Neither do I, but I felt I needed to make an exception this time." Victoria leaned in closer to Teri.

"As long as we are on the same page," Teri said as she also leaned in closer.

Their lips were so close they could feel each other's breath.

"I want to fuck you, Teri, no strings attached. This isn't romance; this is fucking. Period, point, blank."

Victoria's lips pressed against Teri's. Teri took the glass of wine out of Victoria's hand and placed it on the coffee table. Teri caressed Victoria's breast as they kissed again. Victoria's nipples began to poke through her dress.

Teri's free hand made its way down Victoria's body. With the other hand already under her skirt, Teri pulled Victoria's thong down her thighs. Teri stood up. She took Victoria by her hand. Victoria stood up following Teri down the dark corridor in her home.

Teri opened the door to her bedroom. She kicked her shoes off while turning the light dimmer just enough to give them a slight glow. Her California king sat in the middle of the large master bedroom. There wasn't much in the room besides the bed, dresser, and nightstand. The platform bed in the middle was all she ever felt she needed. Teri guided Victoria into the room. She pulled Victoria's body close to her with one quick pull. Victoria fell into her arms, wrapping her arms around Teri's broad shoulders. Teri unzipped the red dress while her lips pressed against Victoria's neck. Victoria pulled each strap down causing the dress to fall to the floor.

Teri took a moment to admire the vision in front of her. She had been with sexy women but Victoria was different. Victoria's dark skin was radiant under the soft glow of the light. Teri ran her hand down Victoria's flat stomach; there wasn't a hair on her. Teri cupped Victoria's butt in her hands, rubbing her lips against the silk on her bra. With one hand Teri unfastened Victoria's strapless bra. It joined the red dress on the floor.

No words were spoken as Teri fell to her knees. She couldn't wait; she had to see if she tasted as good as she looked. Victoria draped her leg over Teri's shoulder as Teri devoured her. She held on to Teri's head as she worked her magic. Victoria let out a soft moan as she ground against Teri's lips. Teri wasn't disappointed.

Victoria's hands massaged Teri's short hair as she sampled all the delight that Victoria had to offer. Teri stood up, picking Victoria up with her upper body strength. She laid Victoria on the bed who took no time pushing Teri's head back in between her legs. Teri pushed Victoria's long legs up in the air as she went in for the kill. Victoria arched her back, wanting to feel Teri as deep as she could.

Teri only stopped long enough to grab her strap out of her bottom dresser drawer. She put a condom on the eight inches of silicone. Teri turned Victoria over. Victoria moaned as she assumed the position on her knees. Teri admired the view rubbing the tip on Victoria before finally entering her. Victoria let out a louder moan. Teri went to work, slapping Victoria's ass in between stokes.

Victoria was obviously no stranger as she twerked against Teri. The sensation was almost too much for Teri to handle.

"I want to ride," Victoria whispered as she pushed Teri down on the bed. Teri lay back on her pillow as Victoria climbed on top. She worked her hips while Teri aggressively massaged her bouncing breasts.

"Shit," Teri moaned at the hurting Victoria was putting on her.

Teri felt a knot forming in her stomach. Victoria ground faster and faster until letting out a loud moan. Her body went limp as she fell on top of Teri, their breasts pushed tightly against each other.

Victoria climbed off and crawled off the side of the bed. "Restroom?"

Teri pointed at the door on the right. Victoria picked up her clothes and headed to the bathroom. Teri didn't know what to think. She wasn't used to women immediately getting up. She unfastened her strap and threw it on the side of the bed. Moments later Victoria appeared completely dressed.

"You don't have to leave you know," Teri said staring at Victoria as she ran her hand across her hair still in the perfect bun.

"I know." Victoria smirked as she walked out of the room.

Surprised, Teri jumped out of the bed and followed. She watched Victoria pick up her purse and shoes.

"This was fun; we have to do it again." Victoria smiled.

"Oh so it's like that?" Teri was amused.

Victoria pulled something out of her purse. She took her thong and put it on Teri's head. "Keep these for me. I'll get them next time."

Victoria opened the front door and walked out leaving Teri speechless and in awe.

Willow heard the key as it went into the door. Katrina walked in the room as quietly as she could. She stopped in her tracks when she saw Willow lying on her side in a baby blue bra and panty set.

"Well hi." Katrina smiled.

"Hello," Willow said in her most sensual voice. "I've been waiting on you."

"Have you?" Katrina dropped her jacket and things by the front door. She unbuttoned her shirt and pulled it off leaving just her sports bra and tank.

"I have, it's just been me and the telly here."

"Well I have to do something to fix that." Katrina pulled her pants off. "I'm going to take a shower. I smell like food.

Katrina disappeared into the bathroom. Willow sat up. She wondered if she looked sexy enough. She wanted everything to be perfect. She tried to think of what Piper would do in this situation.

Katrina let the hot water hit her head. Steam began to fill the bathroom. Willow looked amazing sitting on the bed; she wanted nothing more than to take her right then and there. Katrina closed her eyes. Saura and the incredible dress she had on came into her mind. She felt her heat rising. If nothing else Saura always made her horny.

Katrina jumped when she felt a pair of hands touching her back. She turned around to find Willow standing in the door of the shower completely naked. Willow stepped into the shower. Katrina couldn't resist. She pulled Willow into her, kissing passion into her mouth.

Katrina pushed Willow against the shower wall. The hot water covered them as her fingers entered Willow. Willow moaned for more as Katrina's mouth nibbled on her breasts. Willow wrapped her leg around Katrina as she sexed her. They kissed as Katrina hit her spot. Willow felt her body twitching with each stroke. She wanted to live in that shower with Katrina.

The rest of the night Katrina made love to Willow's mind, body, and soul. Katrina knew that the connection was real with Willow as she ran her fingers through Willow's moist hair. She couldn't deny that she wanted Willow. But as images of Saura filled her mind while lying with Willow, she couldn't help but realize that she still had something with Saura, and she had no idea how she was going to figure out which one she was supposed to be with.

Chapter 17

Katrina kissed Willow on her forehead waking her out of her sleep. Willow turned over to see Katrina standing over her in the clothes she had on the night before.

"Hey," Willow whispered.

"Hey, you. I gotta get over to the restaurant for some press. Devon is going to come pick you up and take you to her house so you aren't in this hotel room."

"She can just drop me at your place. I don't want to be a nuisance."

Katrina froze, she knew that wasn't going to work. "You aren't a nuisance, but I don't want to leave you alone."

"I will be all right." Willow smiled.

Katrina sighed as she sat on the side of the bed. "You have to promise not to overreact."

Willow braced herself.

"Because we shared a house together, Saura went back to the house. But I am going to tell her she has to go today."

Willow wanted to scream. Saura was ruining all the things she had planned with Katrina. She should be in Katrina's house, preparing for another night of pure erotic bliss. Willow remained calm. At least Katrina was in her bed last night; that was a good sign.

"Okay, do whatever you have to do."

"Thank you for being so understanding." Katrina kissed Willow on her forehead.

Willow watched as the woman she was falling in love with walked out the door. She turned the television on and turned to the BBC. It was comforting to have a bit of her home in the foreign town. Willow finally pulled herself out of the comfortable bed. She took a quick shower, thinking about the amazing shower she had the night before.

Willow put on the plush hotel robe and searched for her outfit for the day. There was a quick knock at the door. She peered through the peephole to see Devon standing there. She looked a lot different from the night before. She had on a pair of baggy pants and a loose-fitting T-shirt, and her hair was pulled back in a ponytail.

"Hello, girl," Devon said as she walked in the room. Even her walk was different. There was a slight masculine movement to it.

"Hi. I'm sorry. I didn't know you were going to be here so soon. It won't take me but a moment to get dressed."

"Take your time. Do I need to leave?" Devon asked.

"Oh no, you are fine," Willow said as she pulled the robe off.

Devon couldn't help but stare at Willow's sexy body. Her ass seemed to sit perfectly in the lace boy shorts she had on. Devon understood why Katrina was having such a hard time deciding. Saura was hot, but Willow was just as sexy in a different way.

"So is there anything that you want to do today? We are in downtown so there are lots of things to do."

"No, I don't want to be a bother, plus all the things I care to do I kind of want to wait on Katrina to do them."

Devon felt a little bad. She knew how Saura had to be feeling. "How are you holding up, you know, with everything?"

Willow pulled a sundress over her head. She sat on the side of the bed. "Can I be totally honest?" Willow asked as she pulled a pair of sandals from her bag.

"Of course." Devon admired the cute dress.

"It's so odd. I mean I really like Katrina. There is this connection between us that is unlike anything I've ever experienced. But I know there is major history there with her and Saura. Although she was with me last night, I can't help but think that she still has feelings for Saura."

Devon nodded her head as Willow poured her heart out to her. Deep down Devon knew that Katrina still had feelings for Saura; she was devastated when she left and that's not something a person gets over in a few months. She felt bad for her friend and for Willow, who was now in the middle of a situation no one saw coming.

"I can't really speak on it, Willow, because I honestly don't know. I know that Katrina really does care about you."

The words caused Willow to blush. "That's all I need for now. I mean we aren't together. She isn't my girlfriend. So I guess I just have to put my cards out there and let them fall where they may."

Devon was impressed by the British beauty. She helped her carry her bags out of the hotel room. They waited for the valet to bring Devon's car. Two men stared them up and down, obviously thinking they were together.

"So, Devon, I like this look today. It's very different from yesterday." Willow smiled.

"Yeah, I like to switch it up from time to time." Devon put her Ray-Bans on.

"I like it. Well I like both looks. You can pull them off well."

Devon handed a couple of dollars to the valet as they got in the car. Devon turned down a side street, which ended up taking them by the historic Beale Street. They ended on Main, passing a theater.

"Oh that's playing at one of our theatres," Devon pointed to the marquee's sign for *Book of Mormon.*

"I went to see *Mary Poppins* the last time I was in London," Devon said as they drove down South Main.

"Oh you have been to London?"

"Yes, about a year and a half ago was my last time there. I went with my family."

"Very cool."

"So if you like fashion there are a few trendy spots on this street if you want to maybe check them out. You can also see the National Civil Rights Museum."

"Oh yeah, I read something about that."

Devon shook her head. She didn't expect a woman from London to know too much about Black American History. She parallel parked between two cars. The two got out and walked down the artsy street. They walked into a woman's apparel store where the manager complimented Willow on her dress. Devon was impressed to learn she made the dress herself.

They walked out of the store and headed down the street. They chatted as if they had been friends forever. Willow was very intelligent and knew a lot about fashion. She promised to make Devon a dress for her birthday.

Devon watched as Willow absorbed all she was learning inside of the National Civil Rights Museum. She knew a lot more than Devon expected her to know. Willow told her more about the British slave trade, something they didn't teach much of in the US school system.

They took photos outside the balcony where Dr. Martin Luther King was assassinated, before heading to grab lunch at one of Devon's favorite places on the street. The small restaurant reminded Willow of some of their local cafés.

"So tell me, when was the last time you dated before meeting Tree?"

Willow took a sip of her martini. "I didn't do too much dating before her. I went to boarding school so outside of fooling around with promiscuous girls I didn't do much. At university I met a few girls but none I truly took interest in. I had one boyfriend but that was to make my father happy. It wasn't until he told me he knew I liked girls that I just decided to come on out."

"I totally understand that. My parents are so freaking conservative and big in the community. It took them awhile to warm up to the fact that baby girl might not marry a man."

They both laughed.

"London is a little more liberal than America. I see all the gay rights issues you guys have. It seems positively horrid."

"Yeah, and this is the South so it's twice as bad. People like Teri and Katrina have it much harder at times than me. As a feminine woman I can pass, but Katrina and Teri, it's not nearly as easy. We've had a few run-ins with men before."

"That's horrible. But Teri and Katrina aren't that masculine."

"But any bit of masculine can be too masculine."

"Devon."

The women turned around to see a woman standing at the takeout counter. She pulled her shades off. Willow noticed the change in Devon's energy. She watched as Devon shifted in her chair as the woman walked up.

"Isn't this a surprise?" The woman smiled at Devon. She glanced at Willow giving her a slightly evil eye.

"Shanice, what are you doing down here?" Devon stood up.

The two awkwardly hugged each other.

"What am I doing here? You are in my hood. I am living over in South Bluffs while my house is being renovated."

"Oh, okay." Devon's voice changed. She sat back down in the chair. "Oh where are my manners? Shanice, this is Willow."

"Pleasure to meet you," Willow said flashing a smile as she shook Shanice's hand.

"Likewise. I'm sorry am I interrupting a date?"

Willow watched as Shanice stared at Devon.

"No, actually Willow is dating Katrina."

"Oh." Shanice took it upon herself to sit at the empty chair at the table. "I heard about her opening. I have to try her restaurant soon."

"You should," Devon said folding her hands on the table.

The waitress brought Shanice her to-go order.

"Well, I guess that's my cue. Devon, keep in touch okay? Nice meeting you again, Willow."

Shanice walked out the door, but not before giving Devon one final glance.

"Sooo, an ex I'm guessing?" Willow sipped her drink.

"That obvious?"

"A little." Willow smiled hoping to ease the tension created by Shanice.

"She's the ex, the one who has been around for years but just won't seem to stay gone."

"Ah, that has to be hard."

"Especially since all of a sudden she's back and popping up all over the place. But that's neither here nor there. I have to stay away from her."

"If you think that's best."

The waitress brought them fresh glasses of water. Willow stared at the glass. "Katrina was right, you guys do use a lot of ice in your drinks."

Devon laughed. She knew that in London ice didn't come in soft drinks. "I really like you, Willow. I'm glad Katrina met you."

"Well I'm happy you like me."

Both girls smiled as they continued to enjoy their afternoon.

Chapter 18

Katrina sat in her car in the driveway. She still hadn't completely worked out how to deal with the situation at hand. After the night before she knew she wanted to take the time to really see what was growing between Willow and herself. Saura made her bed, and now she had to lie in it.

Katrina mustered up the strength and headed into the house. Sitting on the couch was Saura with a very angry expression.

"So you just got rid of all traces of me I see?" Saura snapped.

"Sorry; that happened after I saw the photos." Katrina sat on the barstool. She didn't want to get too close to Saura.

"Well, I guess I deserved that. How was your night?"

"Don't ask questions you really don't want to know the answer to." Katrina folded her arms.

Saura stood up. She walked over and sat on the stool next to Katrina. "Tree, come on, are you telling me you really want to be with that girl?"

"I like her. I really do."

"Okay, but like and love are two completely different things."

Katrina sighed. She stood up and walked back to the room they used to share. Saura followed her. Katrina began pulling out an outfit to change into.

"You don't get it, Saura. You chose to leave. What did you expect me to do, sit around and wait on you?"

Saura folded her arms. "No, but I didn't expect you to jump into a relationship with the first Pop-Tart you met."

"It wasn't like that. I didn't expect to meet Willow; the shit was real random. We had a connection. I can't deny that. Hell I spent the whole month with her."

The words cut Saura like a knife. "So you are telling me that you didn't just meet this chick in London, you took her on the rest of your trip with you?"

Katrina could tell it hurt Saura but a piece of her didn't care. She wanted Saura to hurt just as much as she hurt her.

"Saura, how was I supposed to know you were going to come back? You never called me on my cell; you never even gave me your new number."

"I didn't want to hurt you any more than I already did," Saura protested.

"Well someone else was there for me when you weren't."

The two stood in silence. Katrina continued to pick out her outfit while Saura sulked in her corner. Saura didn't know what to say. Truth was, she left, and now she was forced to deal with the reality that she might not get her woman back.

"So are you kicking me out?"

"Saura, you know you can't stay here. Willow came all the way from London. I am not going to make her stay in a hotel."

"So you are going to make me stay in one?"

"I don't know what to tell you, Saura."

"This is utter bullshit. This is our house, hell I decorated everything in there and now you are telling me I can't stay here?"

"Well you never should have left."

Saura threw a shirt at Katrina. Katrina turned around to see the tears rolling down Saura's face. Even though she was upset she knew she couldn't put Saura out on the street.

"Saura, I will go and stay in Devon's guest house with Willow. You can stay here, but you need to find a place to go by the end of the week. No exceptions."

Katrina threw a few clothes in a duffle bag and headed out the door.

Teri knew it was a bad idea to drink as much as she did at the party. Even Ming was filling prescriptions with his shades on.

"Is it me or is the light brighter than usual in here?" Ming leaned against Teri's door.

"It's a bit brutal," Teri said reading over an inventory list.

Ming pulled his shades up, resting them on his head. "So you and Victoria, what happened?"

"None ya." Teri continued to read.

"Bitch, you better spill the tea." Ming sat in the chair next to the desk.

"Don't you have some work to do?"

"Nope, I'm all ears." Ming crossed his arms.

Teri thought about the night. It almost felt like a drunken dream. Victoria was a force to be reckoned with. Teri had never been someone's bitch before; she had to admit she liked it more than she expected.

"We hung out at the party and she went home."

"To whose home?" Ming stared at Teri.

"Ming, I slept alone in my bed last night."

Teri knew that Ming could read her when she lied so she decided to tell a partial lie. Truth was she did sleep in her bed alone. Victoria left as soon as they were finished.

"Well that's tragic." Ming frowned. "I guess there is always next time."

"I guess."

Teri continued to work through the afternoon. Things heated up in the pharmacy causing her to actually help Ming with orders. She decided to take a break to grab a bite to eat at the cafeteria.

Teri decided to sit outside on her lunch break. She took a bite of the turkey club she got from the cafeteria. She put her shades on and closed her eyes, allowing the sun to soak into her skin.

"That looks good. What is it?"

Teri turned to see Victoria standing next to the bench. She sat down next to Teri.

"Turkey club, want a bite?"

Victoria broke a small piece off of the edge of the sandwich.

"What are you doing here?" Teri questioned.

"Well I decided to come and do a little work. I saw you sitting out here and couldn't resist the urge to come mess with you."

"Ah is that what you are doing? Messing with me?"

Victoria smirked. "Yes, among other things. You should stop by my office when you have a free moment." Victoria grabbed Teri's hand. She placed something in it and closed her fist. Teri watched Victoria walk off in her high-priced heels. She opened her hand to find a black lace thong.

Teri knocked on Victoria's office door. She heard Victoria telling her to enter in her most professional voice. Teri closed the door behind her, locking it and pulling the shade down.

They didn't speak as Victoria sat on top of her desk. Teri walked in front of her asserting her body in between

Victoria's legs. Teri's hand grazed Victoria's thigh until reaching its destination. Victoria was more than ready for her, heat pulsated from her legs.

Victoria let out a soft moan as Teri sexed her. Not to be outdone Teri shoved Victoria's thong into her mouth. Victoria body responded with delight at Teri's aggressiveness. Teri didn't care about the bun; she pulled on Victoria's hair until the bun came down. She licked and sucked on Victoria's neck, tempted to leave a passion mark, but knowing that would be highly unprofessional.

Victoria erupted, covering Teri's hand. Teri didn't move, she wanted to feel her until the last drop fell. Victoria panted, trying to catch her breath after the intense orgasm. Teri pulled her hand out, licking the essence of Victoria off of her hand. She took the panties out of Victoria's mouth and wiped her hand with them.

"These go in my new collection." Teri pecked Victoria on her lips before walking out of the room, leaving Victoria stuck in the same position.

Teri arrived back at the pharmacy to find Ming looking stressed.

"Um, where the hell have you been? I could use a little help here," Ming bitched.

"No problem; let me just wash my hands."

Teri walked into their private bathroom feeling a true sense of accomplishment.

Chapter 19

Willow loved Devon's house. The one-story house was very open and spacious but still felt very warm and inviting. But the thing Willow loved the most was the backyard. It was an entertainer's dream. The kidney-shaped pool had a waterfall that hid the grotto, which was also a hot tub. There wasn't much grass, just a few patches in between the pool and the patio area. The lawn chairs were also very plush with thick waterproof cushions. In the middle was a fire pit. Farther back was a completely separate residence that used to be a pool house that Devon remodeled to be a guest house.

"Your house is just amazing." Willow said as she sat on the barstool watching Devon cutting up lettuce.

"Thank you, it's my baby. My parents bought her for me when I graduated from grad school but I did a big remodel on it." Devon was very proud of her house. It was the main thing that kept her living in Memphis. She pulled a tomato out of the large refrigerator.

"Are you sure you don't want me to help with anything?"

Devon shook her head. "You just sit there and enjoy your wine."

The women both turned their heads when they heard a key unlocking the front door. Katrina walked in wearing her chef's jacket. She put her bag down and walked toward the living room.

"What's up, chica?" Devon smiled as her friend walked in the living room.

Katrina kissed Willow on her cheek. Willow's face turned pink.

"Nothing much, things are going good at the restaurant. We are booked for dinner for the next two weeks."

"Damn right." Devon gave Katrina a high five.

Katrina walked in the kitchen to watch what Devon was doing. She checked the fish, which was sitting in a marinade.

"What did you use on this?" Katrina frowned.

Devon pointed at the store-bought marinade. Katrina scolded her as she pulled out a few seasonings and began seasoning the fish. Devon shook her head at her perfectionist friend.

"So what did you think of that chick Teri was with last night?" Devon said handing the knife to Katrina. She watched as Katrina quickly diced the tomato that was taking her forever to cut.

"She seemed a hell of a lot better than the chickenheads she usually dates."

"What is a chickenhead?" Willow asked.

The friends laughed explaining the meaning to her.

"I don't know; she seemed a bit dodgy to me."

"Dodgy?" Katrina and Devon said at the same time.

"Yeah, um like a bit shady."

Both women shrugged their shoulders.

"I guess we need to pay better attention next time we are around her." Katrina continued to cut up veggies.

Devon grabbed her glass of wine. "Whelp, looks like you got this here. I'm going to go prepare the grill." Devon walked out the sliding patio door.

Willow and Katrina smiled at each other.

"How was your day?" Katrina looked at Willow.

"It was nice. We went to the Civil Rights Museum. I learned so much."

"Cool, cool. Did you do anything else?"

"Just a little window shopping. How about you, how was your day?"

Katrina put the knife down. She knew she had to break the news to Willow. She came from behind the kitchen counter and sat on the stool next to her. Katrina held Willow's hands.

"I don't want you to think anything of this, but we are going to stay here at Devon's for the week."

"What's going on?" Willow braced herself.

"Saura and I used to live together. So when she came here she didn't expect that I would have someone else. She didn't have anywhere else to go so I told her she could stay at my place for the week but she had to be gone at the end of the week."

Saura was officially getting on Willow's nerves. She thought of Piper and what she would tell her to do. She didn't see it as a huge threat. Katrina was going to be staying at Devon's with her. That was the most important thing.

"I'm cool. Hell I like Devon's house. I can get an early dip in."

"Maybe even a skinny dip with me." Katrina winked her eye.

The two began to kiss.

"Ugh get a room," Teri said as she walked in the house. She put a bottle of wine on the counter top.

"Where's your date?" Katrina smirked.

"What date?"

Katrina grabbed the tray of fish and the group headed out to the patio. Willow watched as Katrina grilled the fish. Teri and Devon argued about who could cook the best out of both of them. Willow admired the friendship they had. She had schoolmates but no one she was close to outside of Piper.

"So where is Ms. Sexual Chocolate?" Devon joked playfully hitting Teri.

"Why does everyone keep calling her that?"

"Ming said it to me so I thought I'd keep it going."

Teri threw her middle finger up at Devon over the smart comment.

"So, Willow, what is it that you see in my friend here?" Teri said sitting in a chair next to Willow. Devon joined them, sitting across from Willow.

"What's not to see in her?" Willow blushed.

"How did you guys meet?" Devon asked.

"Well Katrina wasn't ready for London weather. It started raining and she ran into the first place she saw. That just so happened to be the coffee shop I was sitting in. We started talking and we haven't stopped talking since."

"Aw, that's so sweet." Devon smiled at Katrina who was grinning from ear to ear while working on the grill.

"I talked her into riding the London Eye with me."

"Wait, this big scaredy-cat got on the London Eye? Get the fuck outta here." Teri sipped her beer.

"Oh she was beyond nervous but she did it. But the funny time was the cliff diving in Italy."

"Okay, who are you and what have you done with my friend?" Devon joked.

Katrina brought the tray of cooked fish over to the group. They each took a piece. "It was horrible. I will never do it again," Katrina said as she sat in the chair.

"I just wanted her to experience some of the things that I love about each country." Willow smiled.

Devon and Teri both noticed the lovesick look in Willow's face. They looked at each other, knowing they had a little bit to worry about.

"It was an amazing experience." Katrina bit a piece of her fish.

"And look, you found a girl in the process," Teri joked.

Katrina flipped Teri off.

"So how long are you going to stay here with us, Willow?" Teri asked.

Willow shrugged her shoulders. "I planned for two weeks but I also didn't plan to go around Europe for a month with her."

"And I didn't plan to spend two extra weeks in London." Katrina smiled at Willow.

"So we are just going to play it by ear I guess." Willow didn't care if she ever left. Memphis was growing on her.

"Well well well, looks like the whole gang is here."

The group turned around to see Saura walking in from the house.

"Saura, what are you doing here?" Katrina stood up.

"Well I missed my friends so I figured I would stop by and join the party. Hi, guys, did you miss me as much as I missed you?" Saura patted Teri on her shoulder. Willow tried not to look at Saura but she could feel her eyes on her.

"Okay, Saura, really, is this necessary?" Devon questioned.

"I think it is. I mean my girl is sitting over here without me. I didn't think that was right."

"I'm not your girl." Katrina walked over grabbing Saura by her arm.

Saura quickly pulled away. "No, I want you all to hear this." Saura stood her ground. "Don't worry, I'm not here to cause a big scene. I just need you all to hear what I have to say."

"What do you have to say, woman?" Teri snapped.

"As I sat in the house that we shared for two years together I realized that this shit right here isn't right. I am not going to just give up my woman without a fight."

"I'm not your woman; you need to roll." Katrina tried to grab Saura's arm again but she jerked away.

"I'm not going to fight you," Willow chimed in. She wasn't going to let Saura get the upper hand again.

"I am not talking about a physical fight." Saura rolled her eyes. "Katrina, you know in your heart you are not completely over me. You may tell that lie to her but you, I, and your friends know the business."

Willow looked at Teri and Devon who were both trying to dodge her glare.

"So I have an idea. Katrina, you want to get to know this girl. Well I feel you should also give me a second chance. So I think you should date both of us."

"Saura, what the hell have you been drinking?" Teri questioned.

"Nothing, but I'll take some of that wine." Saura took Devon's glass off of the table.

"Saura, I'm not playing this game with you. Now you need to leave!" Katrina demanded.

"Wait."

All eyes were on Willow. She sat up in the chair.

"I think it's a brilliant idea." Willow folded her arms.

The group of friends all protested.

"Look, Katrina, you know how I feel about you, but I know I am not going to be completely happy until I know for a fact that you are over her. And the only way for that to happen is if you get all unfinished business out of the way. People date more than one person all the time. You aren't committed to me, so why not test the waters, figure out where your feelings really lie?"

Saura threw her hands in the air. "See, I kinda like this girl already. Katrina, I'm not giving you up that easy. I deserve my time to show you that I mean business."

"This is bullshit," Katrina huffed. "I'm not playing some game. It's not fair to either of you."

"Well, Katrina, to be honest they both do have a point," Teri interjected. "Spend time with both of them; see which one you are more invested in."

"No, I'm not doing this. Willow, why are you okay with this?" Katrina turned to Willow.

"Because I want you to want me and only me, and can you honestly say right now that you don't still have feelings for her?"

The only sound was the sound of the waterfall. Katrina knew it was a bad idea but something also intrigued her about the situation. She could work though her feelings with Saura without hurting Willow in the process.

"I gotta think about this."

"Well while you think I feel like you shouldn't sleep with either one of us. Actually, date us both, no sex involved." Saura sipped the wine.

"No sex, oh hell no, that's a terrible idea after all." Teri folded her arms while shaking her head.

"This whole thing is asinine," Devon huffed. "No one can truly date more than one person. You won't be giving your all to one."

"When you realize the one you want to spend the most time with then you will know who you are supposed to be with. And I have no doubt in my mind that will be me." Saura rolled her eyes at Willow.

Katrina felt like she was stuck between a rock and a hard place. She looked at Willow and Saura who were both staring each other down. Both women were beautiful and she had feelings for both of them. Could this crazy idea actually work?

"I have to think about this," Katrina said. "But as of now you need to go."

Saura finished the glass of wine, placing the empty glass back down. She stood up. "May the best woman win." Saura grimaced toward Willow.

"I'm sure I will."

Chapter 20

Katrina watched as Willow settled into the guest house. She stood in the doorway watching Willow's every move, hoping to see a sign that she wasn't really okay with what happened earlier. "Are you sure you will be all right out here by yourself?"

Willow smiled. It was a good sign that Katrina was so worried about her. "I think I will be just fine."

"Willow, how are you okay with this bullshit?" Katrina sat on the edge of the bed.

Willow joined her, placing her hand on Katrina's thigh. "Katrina, can you look me in my eye and tell me you are completely over her?"

Katrina stared at Willow in her big brown eyes. She sighed; she couldn't answer the question.

"See, I understand because you guys had all that time together. You didn't expect to meet me, and neither of us knew what was going to happen after that day in the coffee shop. You were supposed to take that time to be alone, but instead you were with me. You didn't have time to get over her."

Katrina couldn't argue with what Willow was saying. She knew a piece of her used Willow to get over Saura. But she still couldn't help thinking it was the best thing to happen to her.

"This is crazy. I feel like a total asshole. You came all the way here and you have to deal with this mess. I wouldn't be surprised if you didn't want to deal with me anymore."

Willow placed her hand on Katrina's cheek. "The only way I'm going anywhere is if you tell me to."

Katrina loved the way Willow's lips felt against hers. She wanted to make love to Willow but she wasn't having it. She left the guest house, hot and bothered. Teri and Devon were sitting in Devon's living room watching a rerun of *Girlfriends*. Katrina closed the patio door behind her.

"Looks like you got yourself in quite a bit of a pickle there, love." Teri attempted a terrible British accent.

"Oh my God, what the fuck is happening?" Katrina plopped down on the sofa, covering her face with her hands while her friends got in a hearty laugh at her expense.

"Look, for real, what the fuck kind of magic skills do you have in your tongue that you have these women willing to duel for your raggedy heart?" Teri joked.

"Wouldn't you like to know," Katrina snarled.

"You got damn right I want to know. This is some crazy stuff."

"It's really not that crazy," Devon chimed in. "The whole purpose of dating is to get to know a person to see if you want to take it to the next level. People date multiple people at once all the time."

"That is true," Teri responded. "You aren't with either one of them. You are technically single. Why not play the field? Hell you should have been playing the field anyway after getting out of a long-term relationship."

"Right. You have only been single for what, two, three months?" Devon sipped her wine.

Katrina listened to her friends; the whole thing was actually making sense to her. It was a unique situation but it would allow her the time to figure things out.

"The only thing I don't agree with is the whole no sex thing; what the hell is up with that? How are you supposed to even know which you want without having sex with them?" Teri folded her arms.

"Is that all you think about?" Devon rolled her eyes. "You act like she hasn't already slept with both of them."

"Hmm." Teri rubbed her chin. "Okay, so tell me, Tree, based off of sexual skills alone, right now which on is in the lead?"

"I'm not answering that." Katrina shook her head.

"Oh come on, which one has the magic vagina?"

Katrina threw a pillow at her vulgar friend.

"Come on, you know you know the answer to it." Teri was grinning from ear to ear.

Katrina thought about the question. "That's actually kind of hard to answer. They are both good in different ways." Katrina continued to think.

"What ways?" Devon asked.

Katrina smirked. "Okay, so Saura is sexy as shit, and kinky, too. She will let me do practically anything to her."

"Aww shit I knew she was a freak." Teri rocked back and forth in her chair.

"Yeah, but Willow is sexy as hell. Her body is amazing and she tastes so fucking good. And I'm not sure about her freak meter because I haven't tried as many things with her as I have with Saura."

All three girls laughed. Teri stood up. "Ladies and ladies we have the battle royal. In one corner the Asian Attack Saura, and in the other corner the British Bombshell Willow. Who shall come out victorious?" Teri belted out sounding like an announcer as she fell back in the chair.

Katrina excused herself from her giggling friends. From her room she watched the light in the guest house go out. For her to have two women vying for her attention she sure felt lonely sleeping alone.

Chapter 21

Katrina watched as the health inspector walked through the restaurant with a fine-tooth comb. On top of everything else she had to pass this final inspection for the restaurant to open full time. She didn't think she had anything to worry about, but she felt a bit nervous anyway.

"All right we checked everything and you are good to go." The inspector handed her the sheet with a grade of ninety-nine.

"What is the one point missing for?" Katrina asked.

"Saw a piece of ice on the ground. Watch that," the inspector said and smiled as he left the building.

Katrina high-fived her sous chef as she retreated to her office for a private celebration. Katrina checked the newspapers for articles on the opening. Everyone had amazing things to say, which only made her day go even better.

"Knock knock."

Katrina looked up to see Saura standing in the door. She obviously came dressed to impress. The jeans she had on looked like she painted them on. Her halter shirt only enhanced her already supple breasts.

"What's up, Saura?"

"Well I figured you might get hungry so I brought you food." Saura held up a bag.

"You brought me food, to my food establishment?" Katrina shook her head.

Saura walked in and closed the door. “Well it’s not just any food; open the bag.”

Katrina obliged opening the bag. She pulled out a sandwich wrapped in a greasy wrapper. She couldn’t help but laugh. She knew the packaging well. “What were you doing at Snootys?”

Saura sat in the chair in front of Katrina’s desk. “Remember the first time you took me there? I was absolutely mortified.” Saura smiled.

“Yeah, then you proceeded to eat two of these bad boys.” Katrina laughed as she opened the cheese steak.

“You couldn’t believe I had such an appetite. I told you the black side of me loved to eat.”

Both women laughed. Katrina felt her guard falling down.

“So, Saura, why did you really come back?”

Saura lowered her head. “Los Angeles just wasn’t what I expected,” she mumbled.

Katrina opened the sandwich. She cut it in half and slid half of it in front of Saura. Saura picked it up and took a bite.

“It has to be more than that. It was your dream after all; and don’t say it was because of me.”

“Honestly, Tree, it was because of you.” Saura glanced at her ex. “Don’t get me wrong, Los Angeles was beautiful, the beaches and all that stuff. I even had some gigs lined up. But as I watched those sluts I lived with bring home man after man I realized that I didn’t want that kind of life.”

Katrina found herself hanging on to every one of Saura’s words.

“I was happy here. What we had was special. I always thought I wanted more fame, but honestly the only person I really wanted was you. And now I might have lost the one thing that I want more than anything else.”

Katrina could see the hurt in Saura's face. She watched as Saura fought to hold back tears. Her eyes tightened more than they usually were.

"So this sandwich, it's quite amazing." Katrina smiled.

"Yeah, like always." Saura smiled back.

The two enjoyed each other's company for the first time in a while.

"Be still," Teri said as she stuck her head back under Victoria's skirt.

They were going at it at least once a day in Victoria's office. Teri loved the rush of office sex. She wondered if anyone would ever knock on the door or even try to come in. Victoria was just as kinky. The bigger the risk the more she enjoyed it. She made Teri bring her strap to work so she could fuck her on her desk. She would call her secretary and have her write things down while Teri was sexing her just to see if she could hold it together.

"Oh right there," Victoria breathed as shockwaves pulsed through her body.

Victoria's waves covered Teri's tongue. Teri held her position, wanting to stay in the moment until the very end. As soon as her moment ended Victoria pushed Teri away. In seconds she was sitting back at her desk as if nothing had happened. Teri washed her face in Victoria's private bathroom. She made sure she was presentable before walking out of the room.

"Hey so I was wondering if you wanted to grab a bite at my friend's restaurant tonight?"

Victoria looked up from her computer. "Um, are you asking me out?"

"If you want to be technical I guess. I'm just asking if you wanted to grab something to eat."

"Aw, Teri, you aren't getting serious on me are you?" Victoria pressed her lips firmly together.

Teri didn't know how to feel about the question. She hadn't been in a situation where a woman didn't want anything from her besides sex, literally. She felt a little offended but shook it off. "Dude, it's dinner. I didn't ask you to marry me."

"Let's just stick to what we have going on. No need to rock the boat."

Victoria began typing away at her computer again. Teri walked out of the office, making a mental note not to come back.

Devon sat at the small café table with her head buried inside a home décor magazine. The Arnold Palmer was refreshing, giving her the energy she needed to endure the Memphis heat. She folded back the edge of a page of a piece of wall art she thought would be perfect in one of her guest rooms.

"Well, well, the beautiful Devon here again."

Devon pulled her eyes from the magazine to see Shanice standing in front of her. Shanice smiled as she put her shades on her head.

"Do you really love this place or are you stalking me?" Shanice winked.

"You know I like this place." Devon put her magazine down. "Can you hurry up and move back to Harbor Town so I can eat in peace?"

Shanice put her big purse on the table and sat down in the empty chair. The waitress came out with a menu and asked if she wanted anything to drink.

"I'll take a sweet tea," Shanice proceeded to order while Devon gave her a disapproving look. She handed the menu back to the waitress and settled into the seat.

"What are you doing?"

"I'm about to have lunch." Shanice pulled her phone out.

"Okay, there are free tables inside."

"I don't want to sit inside." Shanice didn't look up from her phone.

"I didn't give you permission to sit here."

"I know." Shanice finally placed her phone on the table. "Do you want me to leave?"

Devon closed her eyes for a moment only to meet Shanice's stare when she opened them, her eyes fixed directly on Devon. Devon noticed Shanice's face was thinner than normal. Her cheekbones were more defined. She knew Shanice wouldn't hesitate to have unnecessary surgery, but this looked natural.

"Have you lost weight?"

Shanice nodded her head. "I've been working out more, yes. Can you answer my question?"

"What question?"

"Do you want me to leave?" Shanice repeated as she continued to stare Devon down. She watched as Devon shifted her body weight, looking off at the trolley passing on the street. Devon turned her head back only to find Shanice still fixated on her.

"Damn it, will you stop!" Devon hit the table. "So fucking annoying."

Shanice laughed. "I always could get you with that." Shanice took the drink from the waitress.

Devon couldn't help but notice Shanice's full red lips as they touched her black straw. Devon suddenly felt a bit hazy; she picked up her drink hoping to cure the lightheaded feeling taking over her body.

"So I say again, Devon, do you want me to leave?"

A devilish grin sprawled across Shanice's face. Devon knew the look well; it was one of her favorite looks.

“Well you have already made yourself comfortable so you might as well stay.” Devon took the moment as a personal challenge. She wasn’t going to allow Shanice to have the upper hand. She could sit at the table with her and feel absolutely nothing for her ex. She was determined: there was no way she was going to fall for Shanice’s charm again.

“So what have you been doing to your hair? It looks amazing.” Shanice sipped her tea.

Devon ran her hand through the blow out. “Thanks.”

“So Katrina met a British chick. She was cute.”

“Yep.” Devon put her shades on.

Shanice huffed. She shook her head. “Okay, Devon, I get it. I am sitting here trying to have an actual conversation with you and all you want to do is give me these short-ass answers. I can take a cue.”

Shanice stood up, pulling her wallet out of her purse. Devon was speechless; she wasn’t used to annoyed Shanice. She watched as Shanice dropped a couple of bills on the table.

“I guess my hope of us being cordial just isn’t going to happen. Have a good day, Devon.”

Devon sat frozen in her place watching Shanice walk across the street and disappear around the corner. She knew Shanice was headed to the condo her parents owned. Devon picked up the bills only to see Shanice’s driver’s license under them. Devon gathered her things and picked up the license. She walked across the street toward the set of condos.

Devon thought about knocking and leaving it on the ground but she knew she couldn’t do that. She pressed the doorbell. She could hear Shanice’s heels clicking against the hardwood floors. Devon took a deep breath as the door opened.

“You dropped this.” Devon held the license up.

Their eyes locked on each other. Shanice grabbed the hand Devon was holding the license in. She jerked Devon into the house pushing her against the wall. Devon's mouth fell as Shanice's lips pressed against her neck. She wanted to speak but couldn't form words. Shanice aggressively pushed her hand under Devon's yoga pants.

Devon wanted to say no. She was screaming no in her head, but she could not make the word come out of her mouth. Devon put her hands on Shanice's chest only to have Shanice push them over her head, pinning Devon's wrists on the wall. Shanice's tongue traced Devon's ear stopping only to nibble on her earlobe.

Devon opened her eyes to see Shanice staring at her, their lips so close they could breathe each other's air.

"Do you want me to stop?"

The deep, seductive rasp in Shanice's voice called out to Devon. It was her moment; all she had to do was say no and she could walk out and still feel good about herself. Her body wanted to give in, but her mind knew it was a terrible idea. As Shanice's tongue grazed Devon's bottom lip she knew there was only one thing to do. Devon tightly closed her eyes and spoke.

"Take me."

Chapter 22

Willow felt something moving on the bed. She opened her eyes to feel arms wrapping around her. A broad smile covered her face as Katrina kissed the nape of her neck.

"What are you doing?"'

"I am kissing you," Katrina whispered as she brushed her lips against the back of Willow's neck again.

Willow couldn't resist the urge to arch her back just enough to press her ass firmly against Katrina. She moved her butt in a circular motion, giggling as she aroused Katrina. Katrina growled, holding Willow tight, her thumb mistakenly grazing Willow's hard nipples. The couple slowly moved their hips in together as Willow's nipple rolled between Katrina's thumb and index finger.

"We aren't supposed to be doing this," Willow muttered.

Katrina hushed her as she buried her head in her wild mane. Willow's body craved Katrina; she wanted it but knew she had to stop. Willow pulled herself away from Katrina getting out of the bed before anything more happened. Katrina let out a loud, disapproving moan.

"You're killing me over here, Willz." Katrina put a pillow over her face.

"So should I get ready to go to Graceland?"

Willow laughed as Katrina moved the pillow from her face to in between her legs. Willow just shook her head as she headed to the bathroom.

Willow let the hot water massage cover her face. Her insatiable hunger for Katrina was reaching epic proportions. She wanted to remain strong, but she wondered how strong she could stay if Katrina appeared in her bed again. It had only been one day and she almost gave in.

Willow explained the situation to Piper who drilled into her to stay on path. She had to make Katrina realize that she was the one she needed to be with. Willow didn't know what was happening to her. She knew it was insane to feel so strongly for someone she had only known for such a short time, but she knew she couldn't deny her heart. Was love at first sight a real thing?

Willow picked up her brush after her shower. She could hear Katrina talking on the phone about food orders. Willow wiped the steam-covered mirror with her hand. She stared at her reflection. Willow pulled her hair back as her insecurities played like a song in her head. Was she as attractive as Saura? Saura had an exotic beauty that she didn't posses. What would make her stand out next to a woman who could easily be a model?

Willow walked out of the bathroom with a large blue towel wrapped around her body. Katrina followed Willow's movements with her eyes. She felt guilty. Lunch with Saura was better than she ever expected. They talked about past things that made them fall in love to begin with. Katrina knew she had a dynamite relationship with Saura up until the end.

Katrina knew she wasn't a saint and she put Saura through a lot in the beginning of their relationship. Before Saura, Katrina was a lone wolf. She was closed to the idea of a relationship just from watching her parents' relationship implode. Also watching Devon cry countless times over failed relationships made Katrina know that she didn't care about the long term, but Saura changed that.

Katrina left the lunch feeling better about Saura than she had in a long time, but those feelings didn't overthrow the feelings she was developing for Willow. Willow was genuine to her core; that was rare in a person. The whole time they spent in Europe was the best time of her life, and she could picture more days like that. The problem was she could picture the future with both women. A future with Saura meant being a beautiful power couple, where a future with Willow meant amazing adventures.

Willow finished getting dressed. She turned around to see Katrina lying on the bed, lost in her own little world. Katrina looked amazing sprawled out across the bed in her jeans and black fitted tank. Willow wondered what was going through Katrina's brain. Was she contemplating their crazy situation or had she already decided on the end result?

"I'm ready."

Katrina turned to see Willow standing in a short fit and flare dress with an hombre effect of a deep blue turning aqua. Her damp curls were pulled off of her face with an aqua-toned headband. Katrina admired her beauty in her simplicity. She didn't have to throw on tons of makeup or tight clothes to look beautiful, she was a true natural beauty.

The couple spent the day acting like tourists. Katrina couldn't believe how much she actually enjoyed Graceland. They held hands as they toured the mansion. Katrina recorded Willow attempting to imitate Elvis to the music playing in the "Gold Room," a room filled with Elvis's gold records and awards. Katrina snapped photos of Willow as she admired all the various artifacts.

"You know I have had hot wings before," Willow informed Katrina as they sat in the small wing joint.

"Please, there is no way possible there are any real hot wings in London." Katrina dismissed Willow with a wave of her hand.

Willow wasn't impressed with the small restaurant. It looked unsanitary, even though the health inspection sign showed a high score. Willow couldn't believe that Elvis's house was in the middle of what she would consider squalor. Elvis Presley Boulevard was filled with fast food restaurants, motels, and tacky Elvis souvenir shops.

The cashier called their ticket number. Katrina grabbed their food and brought it back to the table. The wings were smothered in red sauce. Willow could see the grease in the puddle of hot sauce.

"You have got to be kidding me." Willow winced while Katrina picked up her first wing sucking the sauce off of it.

"Just eat it. What, don't you trust me?" Katrina winked her right eye using Willow's words against her.

Against her better judgment she picked up a wing and broke a piece of the meat off. She closed her eyes and put the chicken in her mouth. The flavor erupted in her mouth. Katrina nodded her head at Willow's wide-eyed expression.

"Oh my God." Willow bit a bigger piece of the wing. "This might be the best thing I have ever tasted in my life."

"I told you, trust me, girl." Katrina continued to eat.

Willow wanted to trust her. She wanted to believe everything was going to work out in her favor. When Katrina was with her it seemed as if she only had eyes for her. Maybe it was true; maybe Katrina was over Saura and only wanted Willow.

"So, Katrina, I don't want to put any pressure on you, but should I be considering extending my trip?"

The question caught Katrina off guard. She wiped the sauce off of her fingers with a napkin. "Do you want to extend your trip?"

"I told you, I want to do whatever it is that you want me to do," Willow responded.

"I'd love if you stayed as long as you would like to."

Willow blushed. "So have you seen Saura?"

Willow regretted the question the moment it came out of her mouth. The change in Katrina's face let her know it was the wrong thing to bring up. They were having an amazing day and she had to bring up the other woman.

"We had lunch yesterday."

The words knocked the wind out of Willow. "Oh." Willow shifted her eyes down toward the greasy pile of wings.

"Willz, are you okay?"

Willow feverishly nodded her head.

"Willow, please don't be upset." Katrina reached out placing her hand on top of Willow's.

"I'm not upset. I signed up for this so it's fine. I mean of course you are going to spend time with her; that's the rules, right?"

The two finished eating in silence. They left the restaurant and got in Katrina's car. The local radio station played R&B music. Katrina drove them over a small bridge. She pulled into a parking lot. She parked so their view was the Mississippi River. Katrina placed her hand on Willow's thigh.

"You remember when we were at the Amalfi Coast and you wanted to do that crazy cliff diving? You told me to trust you and I did, the same way I trusted you on the London Eye and the Eiffel Tower." Katrina's thumb moved back and forth on Willow's thigh.

Willow looked at Katrina who was staring out of the window at the river.

"I'm asking that while you are here please trust me. Your feelings mean a lot to me, Willow. I may not know everything, but I know that."

Willow placed her hand on Katrina's cheek. Katrina pressed against her like a cat, rubbing her face against Willow's hand.

“Kiss me,” Willow muttered in a hushed tone.

Willow could fell her heart pounding as Katrina’s soft lips pressed against her lips. Katrina’s hand pulled her head closer, becoming entangled in her curls. Willow closed her eyes allowing the softness of Katrina’s touch, and the cold, minty breeze from the mint Katrina had recently eaten, to take her to another place. She wanted to preserve that moment in time when nothing mattered but them.

Willow’s body was electrified. Every touch of Katrina’s fingers sent pulses of energy through her body making the tiny hairs on the back of her neck stand up. This had to be real; there was no way someone who wasn’t designed specifically for her could make her feel that way. She couldn’t deny it, and she knew Katrina had to feel it too. Katrina’s phone rang, interrupting their perfect moment.

“I gotta answer this.” Katrina sighed as she pressed answer.

The moment was fading as Willow listened to her on the phone with the restaurant manager. Her heat was cooling; the electric feeling subsided. Willow stared at the muddy river water as it flowed. She wanted that feeling; she wanted to feel the wetness of Katrina on her skin. She wanted to throw the rules out the window, pull her dress over her head, and have Katrina take her right there on the bank of the Mississippi. But she knew she couldn’t. It wouldn’t be right. She hated caring so much.

Chapter 23

Devon opened her eyes and waited as they focused on the large print of *Sunflowers* by Van Gogh on the wall. She knew that painting; she had given it to Shanice as a birthday present a few years back. She turned over to see she was alone in the bed. Devon slapped her hand against her forehead. She did the one thing she forbade herself to do.

The cold hardwood sent chills through her body as her feet touched the floor. She quietly picked up each article of her clothing as she did a shame walk into the bathroom. Devon turned on the light to see her shameful face staring back. She was ashamed of herself.

Devon quickly dressed and walked out of the bathroom. She paused in the bedroom she had spent many nights in years ago. Everything seemed to be the same; Shanice even had the jewelry armoire that Devon purchased for her. Devon noticed a lot of the items in the room were gifts from her. The crystal vase holding tulips and the Victorian-style chaise against the wall. Devon had practically purchased everything in the room.

Devon tiptoed down the long corridor, she didn't hear anything. She wondered where Shanice was. She picked up her bag and put her shoes on. Leaving without seeing Shanice sounded like the perfect plan. At least that way she didn't have to say anything. Devon opened the front door and rushed out.

"Going somewhere?"

The voice startled Devon. She turned around to see Shanice sitting on her patio. The sly smirk on Shanice's face disgusted Devon.

"Were you running away, Dev?" Shanice crossed her arms.

"I have things to do," Devon stuttered.

"Right, well you know where to find me when you want to come back."

The cocky response only infuriated Devon. She stormed over to the patio gate. "First off, this shit never should have happened. You got me this time, but it won't happen again. Stay away from me."

"I can't do that." Shanice stood up.

"Why?" Devon yelled.

"Because, I still love you."

Devon's body tensed. She wanted to scream but she couldn't. She stood there with her lips pressed firmly together. Shanice walked closer; the only thing separating them was the short patio fence.

"I love you, Devon. I know that I fucked up countless times, but I was young and dumb and didn't realize that I had my perfect woman staring me in my face. I can't let you go. I need you. I breathe you. I fucking love you, Devon."

Devon let the words replay in her mind. She searched Shanice's face for a sign that everything she was saying was a lie. For once she actually looked completely sincere. Shanice placed her hand on top of Devon's that was resting on the gate.

"Are you out of your fucking mind?" Devon snapped as she jerked her hand away from Shanice. "You are obviously completely mental. Do you really think that I would fall for your bullshit again? Get the fuck out of here with that shit. You don't love me, you love yourself and you crave what you can't have."

"Devon!" Shanice attempted to grab Devon's hand but she jerked away again.

"Do you know there was a time I would have died to have you say those words to me? All I wanted for years was for you to love me the way I loved you."

"I can do that now, Devon. Please, let me show you."

Devon stood there as Shanice pleaded her case. It was all true; they were young when they started dating and as years went on both of them changed. Shanice argued how a person could change in a month, let alone three years. Tears fell from Shanice's eyes as she begged Devon to come back in the house and let her start making things up to her. Devon listened to every word coming out of Shanice's mouth until Shanice had exhausted every angle she could.

"Please, Devon, just give me a month, or a week to prove to you how much I love you. I'll do anything. Let's go on a trip, Jamaica or Rio. Fuck it, let me put the ring on your finger that I should have put on years ago. Let's just go; it can be me and you, together."

Devon didn't take her eyes off of Shanice as she contemplated the platinum offer. She took a step closer to the gate. Devon tipped Shanice's head up as she lowered her plump lips on hers. The softness of Shanice's lips felt warm against Devon's. It was familiar and comfortable, but also terrifying. An expression of pure bliss covered Shanice's face as they pulled apart. Devon moved her hand from Shanice's chin, resting it on her left cheek.

"Shanice." Devon's sensual voice enticed Shanice.

"Yes, baby."

"Go fuck yourself."

Lips pressed together, a grin appeared on Devon's face as she put her shades on, turned around, and walked away. Once the reality hit Shanice she began to shout.

"Fuck you, Devon, you'll be back!"

Devon smiled as she continued to walk. And as one final gesture she strutted, throwing her hand up in the air, holding her middle finger up the entire way.

Teri pulled into her parking spot at work. The cherry red sports car pulled into the spot next to hers. She stepped out of her car, ignoring how sexy Victoria looked in her convertible. Teri heard the door of the sports car close. She didn't turn around; she knew if she did they would end up back in the car with her hand up Victoria's skirt.

"Hello," Victoria yelled as Teri continued to walk.

"Hello, Ms. Gold," Teri responded without turning around. She didn't stop until she was safely in the building.

Teri greeted Ming who was busy filling an order for a patient. She put on her medical lab jacket and began helping fill the other order that was on the form. She had successfully been ignoring Victoria for a couple of days. Teri didn't mind having a random sex thing with a chick, but she refused to mess with anyone if she wasn't in control.

The door to the pharmacy lab swung open. Victoria startled Ming causing him to drop the pills on the tray. He scrambled to pick the little blue pills up. Teri stared at Victoria, who looked like her head was going to explode.

"May I see you in my office please?" Victoria scowled.

"I'm very busy right now." Teri shrugged her shoulders holding up two bottles of pills.

"Okay, well then we can have this discussion in your office."

Victoria rushed past Ming and into Teri's office. Teri looked at Ming shrugging her shoulders at the scene Victoria just created. Teri put the two bottles of pills down and walked into her office, closing her door behind her. The moment the door closed Ming ran up pressing his ear against the door.

"So because I don't give you the reaction you want you start ignoring me?" Victoria huffed.

"Look, no one talks to me the way you did the other day. I am not your fucking puppet." Teri leaned against her desk folding her arms.

"So that is what this is about? I have called you multiple times and you are acting like a spoiled child who didn't get her way."

"Let me explain something to you. I do what I want, when I want. You don't run shit over here. You might be used to dealing with weak-ass studs who are willing to take whatever you throw at them, but this ain't that over here."

"Is that right?"

"Fucking right." Teri turned her head away from Victoria.

Victoria took a step back. She studied the stiff stance Teri was taking. It was turning her on. "I thought you were okay with just having fun."

"I am, but our versions of fun are obviously two different things. I am not trying to date you, but as two people fucking we should be able to hold a fucking conversation or have dinner without there being stipulations or strings attached."

The two stood like two cowboys at high noon. Victoria's arms dropped to her sides. "Teri, I like fucking you. I don't want it to stop."

"Well I guess we can't always get what we want."

Victoria stomped her red bottoms on the floor. "Oh come on, Teri, you know you want it just as much as I do."

Teri shook her head. "Nah, I'm good. Maybe if you learn how to talk to a person things will change."

Victoria's heels clicked on the floor as she walked closer to Teri. Her breasts brushed against Teri's folded arms. "You are right. I have the tendency to be a little harsh. I promise I will try to work on that."

Teri wanted to keep her guard up but Victoria's perfume was setting her body ablaze.

"Why don't you teach me a lesson?" Victoria breathed passion toward Teri.

With a quick tug Victoria was bent over the side of Teri's desk. Teri raised her skirt, ripping her panties off with her hands. Teri smacked Victoria on her bare brown ass, shoving her hand in between her legs. With her free hand, Teri stuck her two middle fingers in Victoria's mouth. She began to suck on her fingers as if they were the best tasting Popsicle on earth.

"Don't ever speak to me like that again, bitch," Teri growled.

Victoria moaned as she nodded her head up and down.

"Now, tonight you are going to come to my house. I am going to make us dinner then I am going to finish this."

Teri felt Victoria's walls tightening against her fingers. She knew she was about to cum. As Victoria's body began to convulse Teri pulled away.

"Go to work," Teri said walking over to her sink to wash Victoria's essence off.

Victoria didn't move; she continued to lean over the side of the desk. Her whole body was shaking from the orgasm she was about to have. She struggled to gain her composure, her body stuck in a state of limbo from the orgasm that she wasn't able to release.

Victoria stood up, pulled her skirt down, and fixed her clothes. She was pissed. She wanted to curse Teri out, but not as much as she wanted to feel Teri inside of her again. She lowered her head in defeat.

"I'll be there at seven," Victoria whimpered as she opened the office door.

They both heard Ming as he ran back to his counter, pretending to count the same blue pills he had before she arrived. Teri closed the pharmacy office door behind her and looked over at Ming who was fanning himself with a small paper bag. Teri walked over, picking up the two bottles she originally had.

"Um, excuse me." Ming held his index finger up. "I just have one tiny thing I want to say."

"What, Ming?"

"If sex with a woman sounds like that all the time, I'm going straight."

They both laughed as they continued with their work.

Chapter 24

Saura clicked the long lighter until the flame lit. She lit the final candle she could find in the house. Saura paused when she noticed the lights in the driveway. She threw the lighter on the coffee table and ran to the bathroom. She checked herself out in the full-length mirror. She was happy with her look.

The living room looked so good it took Katrina a moment to close the door behind her. White candles were lit all over the place. The coffee table was moved and a blanket lay in the middle of the floor; on top, all her favorite types of sushi and a bottle of her favorite sake.

"*Konnichi wa.*"

"Oh wow." Katrina laughed as Saura pranced out of the bedroom wearing a tight Japanese kimono. "Really?"

"Yes, really." Saura took Katrina by her hand and led her to the blanket.

Katrina kicked off her shoes and sat down on a large pillow. Saura knelt down on her knees imitating the way she saw them do it on *Memoirs of a Geisha*. Saura poured sake in Katrina's small cup.

The couple laughed as they ate sushi. It felt like old times as Katrina listened to Saura talk about her time in Los Angeles and some of the women she lived with. She was especially obsessed with one roommate who ate only carrots for three days straight.

"So tell me about the trip. What was your favorite part?" Saura questioned as she poured more sake in Katrina's cup. Saura smiled when Katrina's eyes brightened.

“It was amazing. I had so many things I loved but I would have to say Rome was my favorite. Just being there felt like I was stepping into the pages of a history book.”

“How was the Coliseum?” Saura asked knowing it was one of the things Katrina wanted to see most of all.

“It was . . . Saura, it was amazing. It of course had issues, but to survive all these years and though a fire and earthquake it was still in amazing condition. They were working to preserve it, but just standing in there I felt like I could hear the crowd roaring for the gladiators. You probably think I sound crazy.”

Saura shook her head. “No, it sounds amazing. I wish I could have experienced it with you.”

Silence fell over the room.

Katrina picked up her cup of sake. “Well, you weren’t there were you?”

Saura hesitated; she didn’t know what to say. She wasn’t there and another woman took her spot. “I can’t apologize enough, Katrina. I was foolish. I thought I wanted something but I was wrong.”

“Saura, something just doesn’t make sense to me. You wanted your shot at fame as much as I wanted to have my restaurant. That feeling doesn’t go away just because you love someone. How am I supposed to know that one day you aren’t going to wake up and realize you still want to chase fame?”

“Because, I won’t. Katrina, fame, fortune, none of that means anything if you don’t have someone to share it with.” Saura sat up on her knees. “I don’t care about it anymore. All I care about is you.”

“But can you blame me for questioning you? Saura, you left me. You didn’t say we could work it out. You didn’t give us the chance to try a long-distance relationship.”

“That’s because I didn’t think it could work. Seldom do long-distance relationships work and you know this.”

"But you didn't even try!" Katrina felt the anger coming back. "Saura, I would have tried to make it work. You didn't give me the chance. You treat me like we are some broke bitches who can't afford a fucking plane ticket. I would have done anything to make us work!"

"Then why aren't you trying to make it work now?" Saura jumped up. "You are sitting here telling me how you would have done anything to make us work, but the second you meet some new girl you are questioning all of our love and our whole relationship."

Katrina stood up. "That's not fair and you know it."

"Why isn't it fair?" Saura walked closer to Katrina. "You caught feeling for this girl after a month. One freaking month! Do you know how that makes me feel, to know I'm that easily replaceable?"

The silence was back. The women stared at each other, neither knowing what to say next. Katrina sat down on her sofa. She put her elbows on her legs, clasping her fingers together over her face.

"Saura, I hate that you feel anyway about Willow. I didn't go to Europe looking to replace you, just like I didn't expect you to show back here. Things happen. We can't control everything."

"I know, Katrina, I know everything you are saying. But I also know if you search inside of you the feelings you had for me are still there."

"I'm not saying I don't still have feeling for you because I do. But I can't deny I have feelings for Willow as well."

The words sliced through Saura's heart. She sat down on the couch next to Katrina, trying to hold back the tears forming in her eyes. Saura felt she was losing the woman she loved. She pulled the ribbon holding her kimono together.

"Well, tell me something, Katrina." Saura stood up. "Do you really not want this anymore?"

Katrina saw the silk fall to the ground out of the side of her eye. She didn't want to turn her head. The beast inside of her was trying to come out, and she needed to keep him tame. Saura walked closer. She picked Katrina's hand up and placed it on her flat stomach. Katrina turned her face to see Saura standing in her birthday suit in front of her. She was the vision she always was.

"Saura, we aren't supposed to do this," Katrina muttered with all the strength she had.

"We are grown people, in our house. We can do whatever we damn well please. Take me, Katrina."

The beast broke out of the cage. Nothing else mattered as she pushed Saura down on the couch. She couldn't think straight. She was on an erotic high and the sake didn't help the situation. Saura's leg draped over Katrina's shoulder as she sucked on her supple breasts. Their mouths met, dancing the familiar dance only they could do together.

Katrina's hand found refuge inside Saura. It felt like she was home, in a place she missed for a very long time. Saura nibbled on Katrina's earlobe, breathing soft moans into Katrina's ears. Katrina closed her eyes; she saw a kaleidoscope of colors in her mind as she took the woman who she loved for so long.

Saura's body twitched as lightning jolts hit her with each stroke. She arched her back, allowing Katrina to reach the deepest depths of her. Her essence flowed like lava trickling down on Katrina's fingers and hand. Katrina felt her body betraying her. She trembled, closing her eyes as tight as she could as she came in unison with Saura.

Willow's face appeared in Katrina's head.

She opened her eyes. She was on top of Saura who was still biting her lip from their moment. Katrina's head was spinning. She slowly got up, holding on to the side of the couch as she gained her balance. Katrina staggered to her bedroom leaving Saura on the couch.

She closed the bathroom door and locked it. The last thing she wanted was Saura coming in for seconds. Katrina looked at her reflection.

Fuck fuck fuck.

She hit the side of her head. Her head was still spinning. She made a mistake and she knew it. Katrina couldn't get Willow out of her head. She made a promise that she broke after a few cups of sake. Where was her willpower? Did Saura have that tight of a hold on her that she couldn't control herself around her?

Katrina swished cold water on her face alerting all of her senses. She took a shower to wash off any evidence of what just happened. She threw her robe on and walked out of the bathroom to see Saura lying across the bed, still completely naked. Suddenly Katrina wasn't enticed anymore. She walked over to her closet.

"Come on, baby, you aren't stopping on me yet?" Saura said playfully spreading her legs. She watched as Katrina threw on a pair of jogging pants and a T-shirt.

"I have to go." Katrina put her watch on and her phone in her pocket.

"What do you mean? Katrina, come on." Saura sat up. "Don't tell me this is because of her?"

"I just gotta go."

Katrina walked out of the bedroom despite Saura's protest. She didn't want to go to Devon's because she couldn't see Willow yet, and she knew she couldn't stay there. She got in her car and just drove.

Chapter 25

"Are you going to tell her?" Devon asked as she, Teri, and Katrina rode down the Green line.

"I don't know what I am going to do. I feel awful. I really do."

"Well she knows something is up. You haven't spent the last two days with her and she's not stupid. There's only so much time you can spend at the restaurant."

"I know." Katrina sighed. "I just don't know how I am going to tell her that I fucked Saura. That was the only rule."

"Well I said it was a dumb rule to begin with. Hell if it was me I would have a threesome with the both of them. Whoever you find yourself wanting to fuck the most is the winner." Teri laughed.

"See there's my issue with the whole thing," Devon interjected. "It's turned into some competition for your heart. This isn't some stupid reality TV show; this is real life. What are you going to do, hand the winner a freaking rose?"

The group pulled off to the rest point. They sat at one of the tables.

"I knew it was a bad idea to begin with. I don't know why I agreed."

"Because you are selfish dog." Teri casually sipped from her water bottle.

"What the fuck do you mean I'm selfish?"

Devon and Katrina looked at Teri.

"Come on, Tree, do you really believe you can't chose between the two? You are over here agonizing about telling Willow about Saura when you are single and free to do what you want. That lets me know you are really feeling Willow."

"Yeah, but what if it's just the newness of Willow that's enticing her? Saura is old news; she's been there and done that. Willow is fresh, new, and still essentially a mystery," Devon added.

"I am not trying to be selfish but yeah, a piece of me likes having both women there for me. Who the hell wouldn't?"

"Well why not admit that to the both of them and continue to date them both? Maybe you could have sister wives." Teri smirked.

"I know one thing: all your drama is becoming exhausting. I'm playing tour guide to your exchange student all damn day, doing things you were supposed to do with her. You should have seen her face yesterday. She did not want to be at the zoo with me."

"I know. I'm sorry about that, Dev." Katrina was ashamed of her actions.

"Yo, and not to mention this whole fucking bike ride has been about you and your women. Have you asked either of us how our love lives are going?"

The women looked at each other.

"You are right, Teri, how is your love life going?" Katrina said sarcastically.

"For your information I am having the best sex of my life. Victoria just can't get enough. This week has been fucking amazing. Every day we are fucking at my house, her office. I'm leaving her ass print all over that hospital."

"Ew." Devon frowned.

"Okay, but what else? Is all you're doing is fucking?"

"You gotdamn right. No strings attached and it's amazing." Teri poked her chest out.

"So let me get this straight." Devon stood up. "You are finally messing with an intelligent, well-off, professional, and beautiful woman and all you do with her is fuck her?"

"But you can move the ratchet bitches in your house and shit."

Katrina and Devon laughed.

"What are you trying to say?" Teri folded her arms.

"I am saying," Devon said, looking at Teri, "that when you finally meet someone who you could be equally yoked with you turn her into a booty call. Did you ever think that maybe you should try to get to know Victoria, maybe actually date her?"

Teri didn't know how to tell her friends the truth. Even if she wanted to date Victoria it was out of the question. They had a specific thing going and it was too late to change in the middle of the game. "Maybe I don't want to be equally yoked with anyone. Tree thought she was all yoked and now she's in a love triangle, and when was the last time you even tried to yoke anyone?"

"I don't think you are using the saying right anymore," Katrina pointed out.

"It doesn't fucking matter," Teri hissed. "What is so special about being in a fucking relationship? I don't see relationships being the best thing since sliced bread for either one of you."

Devon and Katrina both lowered their heads. Teri was right; relationships hadn't worked out in their favor.

"Look, I may not have found the right person but I do believe that there is someone out there for me. I'm not going to dismiss a person just because I don't want the work that falling in love can take." Devon took another sip from her water bottle.

"Okay well, Katrina, it's the end of the week. You have been out with both girls. If you had to choose one today who would it be?"

Teri's question brought all eyes on Katrina.

"I . . . I don't know."

"Well, Tree, maybe you should take some time to figure that out." Devon patted her friend on her back.

The trio got back on their bikes to continue the trail. Katrina couldn't stop her mind from racing the entire way.

Willow dove into Devon's warm swimming pool. She stayed under, opening her eyes. The blue water had a calming effect on her. She swam up to the waterfall, climbing into the hidden grotto. Willow let the sound of the waterfall calm her nerves. She had only seen Katrina in passing in the last two days. She knew she had dinner with Saura, and it was killing her that she didn't know what happened. She wondered if she was really busy at the restaurant, or if she was avoiding her.

The whole situation was wearing on her spirit. Piper kept telling her to fight for what she wanted, but she wondered how much fight she had left in her. Although her heart was telling her that Katrina was the one, her brain was calling her an idiot daily. How could she be so invested in someone she had only known for a little over two months?

"I'm going to get her."

Willow opened her eyes when she heard Katrina's voice. Willow perked up. She rushed out of the grotto and swam to the pool steps. Willow ran to the guest house to find Katrina standing in the room.

"Hey, I was wondering where you were," Katrina said as Willow walked into the house wiping the water from her with the towel.

"I just decided to take a dip in the pool. What's going on?"

"We are going out tonight." Katrina smiled.

A huge smile covered Willow's face. The truth was she didn't want to spend another day kicking it with Devon. Willow thought Devon was sweet, but she didn't come all the way from London to hang with Katrina's best friend.

Katrina sat on the bed contemplating her next move. She didn't know if she should tell Willow what happened. The last thing she wanted to do was hurt Willow. Katrina decided to take a page from Teri's book and keep the little incident to herself.

Willow decided it was time to take Piper's advice. She pulled out her sexy black peasant dress that was so short she knew she had to watch it bending over. The dress hung off her shoulders, with only two small strings holding the dress up on her shoulders. The crystal embellishments on the bottom added an elegant touch to the flirty dress. She put on a pair of open-toed stiletto boots Piper gave her. Willow infused her hair giving her huge curls.

Katrina turned her head from the television when Willow walked out of the bathroom. Katrina sat up in the chair; she did a double take; her eyes widened at the vision standing in the bathroom. Willow was always beautiful, but she pulled out all her sex appeal in the dress. Katrina felt the heat rising. She didn't want to take her out; she wanted to keep Willow all to herself.

"What do you think?" Willow asked the drooling Katrina.

"I . . . I . . . um," Katrina stuttered. "I . . . wow."

Willow smiled. She had to remember to thank Piper later.

They walked into the main house to see Teri nursing some cognac on the couch. Devon walked out of the bedroom wearing a short black skater dress with a plunging neckline. She stopped in her tracks when she laid eyes on Willow.

"Damn, bitch, I need to go change," Devon said looking at Willow up and down.

Katrina stood behind Willow. She wrapped her arms around her torso. Teri turned her head to see Willow. Her mouth dropped open.

"Fuck why does this bitch get all the hot girls?" Teri stood up, taking the last of her drink to the head.

The group headed to one of their favorite lounges. The cover band was live, packing the dance floor with people two stepping to the beat. The group made it to their reserved table where a bottle of Grey Goose was sitting on ice.

"Willow, come on, girl, let's dance." Devon stood up.

"You better keep the men off of her, Devon," Katrina warned.

"Hey you snooze you lose," Devon yelled as the two headed to the dance floor.

Katrina watched as Devon showed Willow the basics of how to two step. The band went into a cover of "Baby I'm Scared of You," which only filled the floor more. Willow made her way back to the table while Devon danced with an attractive bald brother.

"I don't know any of these songs," Willow said as she sat on Katrina's knee. "But I like it."

Katrina kissed Willow on her cheek as they moved to the music at the chair.

Teri headed to the bar to grab something to mix in the Grey Goose. She rolled her eyes, annoyed with the bartender who kept bypassing her for men she felt would tip better. Teri turned around to check out what was happening on the dance floor. She noticed a face that looked too familiar.

Teri made her way through the crowd. She was right; toward the stage was Victoria dancing with a tall white man. Teri couldn't help but laugh at the man who was struggling to keep up with Victoria. Teri walked over tapping Victoria on her shoulder. Vitoria turned around. Her expression was quite haunting.

"Hey."

"Um hello, Ms. Teri. Daniel, this is Teri Howard, she works in pharmaceuticals. Teri, this is Daniel, my husband."

Teri wanted to blow the spot up but she resisted the urge. She held her hand out, shaking Daniel's hand. Victoria clung to Daniel's jacket for dear life.

"Well I just wanted to come over and say hi. I thought it was you I saw." Teri looked Victoria in her eyes. She wanted her to know she was pissed.

"It's great seeing you. I will see you at work Monday."

"Yes, you will." Teri walked away.

Willow noticed a man staring at her and Katrina. It wasn't the usual stares she got for being sexy. This man looked like he was angry about something. Devon came back from the dance floor and plopped down in her seat just as Teri arrived with a tray of glasses with cranberry juice in them. Willow glanced back at the man; he was staring at her, folding his arms. Uncomfortable, she slid off Katrina's knee and into her own chair.

"What's wrong," Katrina asked as Willow's energy seemed to shift.

"Nothing, I'm all right."

Katrina turned her body completely to Willow who wouldn't stop looking down at the table.

"It's nothing." Willow shook her head.

"No, Willz, tell me."

Willow motioned her head in the direction of the man. "I am probably overreacting but he just kept staring and it made me feel weird."

Katrina slowly glanced at the guy who was making no attempt to hide his distaste for their table.

"Just try to ignore him but if you feel uncomfortable we can leave."

"No, I'm okay. It's nothing; I am sure of it." Willow smiled; the last thing she wanted to do was ruin the night before it really got started.

The club reached maximum capacity. Teri felt like a fool but she couldn't stop staring at Victoria and her husband. How did she not know the woman was married? There were no signs of a husband in her house or office. She never wore a ring and never mentioned anything about any type of partner. Teri felt some kind of way as she continued to stalk the couple through the club. She took her moment when she saw Victoria heading to the bathroom.

Victoria came out of the stall to see Teri staring at her through the mirror. Victoria walked up to the sink next to Teri. She began washing her hands.

"I know you are mad," Victoria said as she lathered the foaming soap on her hands.

"I'm not mad." Teri shook her head. "I'm fucking furious."

"Teri, you can't be that mad. We aren't in a relationship or anything. Well we've been fucking for a week."

"It's not about what we have been doing or how long we have known each other. You lied to me."

"I didn't lie. I omitted." Victoria showed no signs of remorse.

"Did you ever think that maybe I didn't want to sleep with a married fucking woman?"

Victoria shrugged her shoulders. "Exactly. If I would have told you we wouldn't have had fun this week. But we did and we still can." Victoria tried to put her arms around Teri who quickly pulled away.

"Okay, you are trippin'. I'm so done with you." Teri turned to walk away until Victoria called her name.

"Teri, this isn't over. You will want me again, and I'll be waiting, with open legs."

Teri shook her head and walked out of the bathroom.

Devon and Willow were completely wasted. The women draped their arms on each other.

"Katrina, I like her, keep her," Devon slurred.

"Okay, I think you are cut off," Katrina said taking the glass from Devon.

"You know I'm right. She's so cute and sexy." Devon held both sides of Willow's face. "Look at this face; you could just kiss her."

Without saying a word Devon leaned in, pressing her lips against Willow's. Katrina's mouth dropped open. Willow was astonished, not sure of what she should do. Devon pulled back with a drunken smile on her face.

"I think I'm going to throw up now." Devon sluggishly stood up. Katrina held on to her friend.

"I'm going to walk with her. I'll be right back," Katrina said to Willow. Willow nodded as she shot the last of her drink.

Willow watched the band and the people dancing on the dance floor. It was different from the dance clubs she went to in London. The old school music had a bluesy vibe that she enjoyed but was new for her. Willow nodded her head to the beat until she felt someone sit down in the seat next to her. She turned her head to see the man who was staring at her earlier.

"I'm sorry but this seat is taken." Willow was nervous. She didn't know what the man was going to try.

"Now you know you are too fine to be a dyke." The man's breath smelled like weed and hard liquor.

"Excuse me, but I would like for you to leave now."

"Aw don't be like that. I'm just letting you know you got better options." The man touched her on her thigh. Willow jumped up from the table.

"Please leave my table immediately," Willow forcefully commanded, which only upset the man more.

"What you too good for a real man?"

Teri appeared. She put her arm in front of Willow. "Come on, Willz, it's time to roll." Teri took Willow by her hand.

The man grabbed Teri's arm. "I ain't done talking yet."

"Let go of me, bro," Teri demanded.

"Fuck outta here." The man pushed Teri with so much force she fell to the floor. Willow helped her up.

Pissed, Willow pushed the man who jerked her by her arm.

"Don't ever put yo' hands on me," the man yelled, shoving Willow in her head until she fell over the chairs.

Two men close by pulled the guy back as Teri helped Willow up. They watched as one of the men argued with the drunk man until he pushed the guy causing him to punch the drunk man, knocking him to the floor with one punch. Security arrived out of nowhere, dragging the unconscious man out of the club.

"Hey are you all right? Are you two all right?" the man who came to their rescue asked.

"Yeah, I think we are okay," Teri replied as she checked on Willow.

Katrina and Devon walked out of the bathroom. They noticed the crowd gathered around their area. Feeling that something was wrong they fought their way through the crowd.

"What happened?" Katrina ran up putting her hands on Willow's shoulders.

"It's okay. The fucking prick pushed me."

"Who fucking pushed you?" Katrina was filled with rage.

"Dude, it's okay. They kicked him out."

"Thank you, sir, for helping." Willow shook the man's hand who came to her rescue.

The group thanked him immensely and sent a bottle over to his table before heading out of the club. They saw the man still surrounded by the police. One of the security guards checked to make sure Willow was all right.

The group walked into Devon's house. Devon sat down at the first chair she could get to. Willow watched as Katrina walked past them without saying anything and headed straight to the guest house.

"Thank you, guys, I had a lovely time." A tight smile covered Willow's face.

"Yeah, right," Teri said as she made herself comfortable on the couch, grabbing the throw blanket off the back and covering herself with it.

"No, I really did; it was rather exciting. Thank you again for taking up for me." Willow patted Teri on her shoulder before exiting the room.

Willow could see Katrina sitting on the edge of the bed, deep in thought. She walked in, pulling the uncomfortable shoes off and flinging them to the side.

"You must put some of that music on my playlist. I can have a Memphis playlist." Willow smiled trying to break through the tension in the room.

"Are you really okay? Let me see your arm."

Willow sat on the bed next to Katrina. Katrina examined the scrape on her arm. She got up and grabbed a bottle of peroxide from the bathroom. She let a little bit of the liquid drop on Willow's arm causing tiny bubbles to appear. Katrina blew on the scrape. The air was cool, causing Willow's body to shiver.

"I'm really okay, Tree. Don't be upset." Willow placed her hand on Katrina's thigh.

"I am mad at myself. I should have been there. I can't believe I wasn't able to protect you."

“You were taking care of your friend, which was just as important. I was okay.” Willow rubbed her hand against Katrina’s thigh.

“I still should have been there.” Katrina’s eyes blurred. The idea of anything happening to Willow was maddening to her.

Suddenly she could see clearly again. She truly did care about Willow, so much the idea of anything happening to her scared her. She knew in that moment that she didn’t want to lose her.

“Willow,” Katrina muttered under her breath.

“Yeah,” Willow replied as she stood up.

“It’s you. I want to be with you.”

Willow couldn’t believe what she was hearing. Katrina stood up, walking over to her surprised girl. Katrina had lifted Willow’s chin with her finger, pressing her lips against Willow’s. Katrina pulled Willow’s body into hers. Nothing else mattered; she wanted to be with Willow more than ever.

Katrina traced the edges of Willow’s body with her fingertips, tasting the salty sweetness of her skin, getting lost in her curves. Their bodies intertwined, becoming one as they gave themselves to each other unconditionally.

Chapter 26

Katrina had never been so sure about anything in her life. Willow was the one she wanted to be with. As they woke up, bodies tangled together, she knew that fate brought them together, and even though she would always care about Saura, her heart no longer belonged to her.

"So you know Teri is expecting something awesome for her birthday," Devon's voice echoed through Katrina's car speakers bringing Katrina out of her own thoughts.

"I know, things are set, we are doing dinner at the restaurant. I am preparing a special meal for us, all her favorites. Do you think we should invite the Victoria chick?"

"I don't know," Devon responded. "You know she might want to find some new booty that night."

Katrina pulled on her street. She let out a loud sigh.

"Oh what's that all about?" Devon questioned.

"I just hope this girl doesn't do anything crazy," Katrina said as her house came into view.

"I mean you know she is going to be mad, but what's the worst that could happen?"

Silence filled the car. They both knew that things could go really bad. Katrina pulled into her driveway.

"Oh I really don't want to do this."

"You got to," Devon's voice echoed through the car. "Go ahead and get it over with."

"If I call you back you better answer the fucking phone. I might need you to call the police."

Devon laughed but Katrina knew she was dead serious. She knew Saura had a mean streak in her; she just hoped she didn't let it out today. Katrina turned her car off and got out. She headed to the front door. She put her key in the door, turning the knob as slow as she could.

Saura came from the back of the house when she heard the front door close. She wasn't expecting Katrina 'til later. As she walked closer and saw the look on Katrina's face, she knew something bad was coming.

"Saura." Katrina stood in the doorway. "We need to talk."

Saura shook her head. She didn't want to hear whatever it was that Katrina wanted to say to her. She could tell from the straight-faced look on Katrina's face what was about to happen, and she wasn't ready for it.

"Saura, please, sit down."

"No, I'd rather stand." Saura stood in the hallway entrance with her arms folded tight.

"I don't really know how to tell you this, but—"

"No, I don't want to hear it. I don't want to hear that you are leaving me for her."

"It's not that I'm leaving you for her, but, Saura, I just don't think this is going to work anymore."

"That's bullshit!" Saura hit her hand against the wall.

Katrina knew things were going to get worse. She braced herself for the meltdown.

"Don't you walk in here and tell me that you are leaving me. No, I don't accept that. I won't."

"Saura, you left me!" Suddenly the familiar anger filled Katrina's body. "You popped back up and yes, I really did think very hard about giving this a second chance but the truth of the matter is you left, you gave up on us, and I moved on. Period, point, blank."

"You don't just move on like that. You can't do this to me. I came back here for you. I gave up my agent and a career I could have had for you."

Katrina shook her head. "You didn't give up for me. You gave up because things weren't going the way you expected. You really expect me to believe that if you would have landed some dream role that you would have thrown that opportunity away for me?"

Saura paused. She didn't want to admit the truth. She did hate Los Angeles and she hated going on cattle call auditions where there were hundreds of other girls just like her. In Memphis she was sought after, she was the *it* girl. In Los Angeles she was just another face in the crowd.

"Katrina, please, it's me. This is us. We built this life together. You can't throw it away; don't do this."

Saura rushed up to Katrina. She grabbed her arm. Katrina stood still, her feet planted firmly on the ground. The tears streaming down Saura's face didn't have the effect that Katrina thought they were going to have. She knew for sure in that moment that she was completely over Saura in that way.

"Saura, please, can we try to part ways on good terms? I will help you get your own place and everything. I don't want you to hate me."

"You don't want me to hate you?" Saura cocked her head to the side.

Katrina watched as Saura paced the floor. She finally sat down on the couch without saying a word. Katrina felt uneasy as she watched Saura staring into space. She didn't want to say anything, fearing she might blow up.

Saura suddenly looked up at Katrina. She nodded her head up and down, over and over again. Her legs were shaking. She pulled her hair back into a ponytail. Katrina wondered if she was about to try to fight her. She pulled her cell phone out just in case she needed to call Devon real fast.

"You know what, fine. I'm not about to do this with you." Saura stood up. "You want to be with the bitch, go be with the bitch. But know something: I am done. Do not come crawling back to me when you realize that she isn't all you expected her to be. There will never be another woman as good as me."

Katrina didn't know what to think. Saura went from ten to zero in a minute. Katrina didn't move from her spot. She couldn't say anything. Saura had the right to be pissed.

"I know you don't want to hear this but I really do care about you and I will always. I hope one day you can come to realize that I never wanted to hurt you."

Katrina stood there for a moment as she watched Saura move about as if nothing had happened. She didn't respond; she just casually walked back to the bedroom. Katrina thought about going back to check on her, but decided it was best to take her exit.

Katrina quickly left the house. She got in her car and pressed Devon's name as soon as her Bluetooth connected to the car.

"Do you need police?"

"I don't think so." Katrina sat in the driveway staring at her door. She expected Saura to come running out with a baseball bat.

"She took it okay?" Devon questioned.

"I honestly don't know what to make of it. But I'm getting the hell out of here before she changes her reaction."

Katrina drove off, staring at her house in the mirror just to make sure she didn't see anything crazy.

Teri watched her ceiling fan spinning slowly around. She hated that Victoria was still on her mind. In one week a woman managed to get under her skin; things like that didn't happen to her. While her friends mocked her for her choices in women, Teri knew the reason she chose to date the women she did. She knew she would never want to settle down with the ratchet girls she dated. They were in and out and that's how she liked it.

Victoria was different. She had all the things she would want if she were to ever really date a woman. She didn't want to admit it, but she did fantasize about having something real with Victoria one day. Teri allowed the possibility of a real relationship enter her mind. She opened her own Pandora's box and now she needed to find a way to close it.

Teri suddenly felt weak; she felt as if she wasn't herself. She allowed Victoria to break the confidence she had in herself. Teri thought about it: yes, Victoria was sexy and powerful, but in the end she was just another woman. She knew she just had to keep telling herself that.

Maybe it was the fact that she was turning thirty-three in a few days that had her on edge. Was she finally getting the itch for a sense of normalcy in her life? Why didn't she crave a relationship the way her friends did? Maybe deep down she wanted to come home to someone. Teri shook her head; she didn't want that. Did she?

She climbed out of bed and walked to her kitchen. Her refrigerator was almost bare. She had been living on fast food and take out for a while. Even the meal she had with Victoria was delivered by her favorite Chinese place. She picked up her phone; she realized how bad it was that she knew the delivery restaurant's number by heart.

An hour later her doorbell rang. She grabbed her wallet and headed to the front door.

"Hey," she said opening the door while trying to simultaneously pull money from her wallet.

"Hello."

Teri looked up to see Victoria holding her takeout bag.

"Don't worry. I already paid for you." Victoria smirked.

Teri grabbed the bag from her. She held up twenty dollars. "Keep the change; and you can go too." Teri leaned against her wall.

Victoria's devilish grin only infuriated Teri. How dare she act smug toward her?

"Oh, Teri, don't be like that, love." Victoria walked past Teri and into her living room.

Teri couldn't believe the audacity of Victoria. She watched as she switched in her short shorts that were hugging her ass just right. Teri shook the erotic thoughts out of her head. She was going to finally put this woman in her place.

"All right so obviously I let you get away with this shit a little too much. But this showing up at my crib and thinking that you are running anything dealing with me is about to end right now." Teri walked into her living room.

Victoria picked up a bottle of wine from her wine rack. She read the label, nodding her head in approval of the rare bottle of wine. "This is nice. Why haven't we drunk this yet?"

"Are you crazy? Seriously? Because I'm really starting to think you are bat shit crazy." Teri took the bottle from Victoria and sat it back on the wall.

"Oh come on, Teri, don't spoil everything. We were just starting to have fun."

"I don't have fun with bitches who get dick on the regular," Teri calmly said as she tried to ignore Victoria's fragrance that was working a number on her senses.

"Touché." Victoria nodded her head again. "I guess I deserved that."

Teri sat on her couch. She wasn't going to back down. But Victoria was looking very sexy in the tight pants and the little black tank looking like a backup dancer in Beyoncé's "Crazy in Love" video.

"Okay so yes, you are right, I was wrong for not telling you. I just saw you and knew I had to have you. I want to keep having you. Why does this little thing have to affect what we have? I mean we were just fooling around."

Teri knew Victoria made a valid point. It wasn't as if she had never messed with a married woman before. The married ones were always the easiest because they would have to always go home afterward. "The difference is you didn't give me the option. I don't play that shit. What if your husband would have caught us?"

"That would never happen."

"How do you know it?"

Victoria sat on the couch next to Teri. "Well for one he still lives in Atlanta. He's a surgeon at Emory." Victoria put her hand on Teri's thigh which Teri immediately moved. "Second I am very careful with what I do."

Teri's head cocked to the side. "What you do? Oh so this is some regular stuff for you. Tell me just how many women are you fucking at the hospital?"

Victoria pushed Teri. She didn't mind the attitude but she wasn't going to allow her to treat her like she was some type of slut.

"Okay so I get that you are mad, but can you please stop acting like a jealous bitch?"

"What did you just call me?" Teri's head snapped around at Victoria.

"You heard me. In the end, Teri, we are just fucking. I picked you because I thought you could handle that. I mean what did you think was going to happen? We were going to fall in love? Ha!"

Teri didn't know why Victoria's comment made her feel like shit. Teri wanted to smack the smug grin off of her face. "First off, fuck you, and second off, you say that that shit as if I am some kind of bullshit, nothing-ass chick. Plenty of women would be more than happy to be with me."

"I'm not most women," Victoria replied.

"What makes you so different?"

Victoria stood up. She stared at Teri who truly didn't see the point she was trying to make. "Teri, okay. Yes, you have a nice thing going here, but seriously, look at me. I graduated top of my class from Yale Medical School. I am currently considering positions from some of the top medical facilities in the country."

"Are you trying to say you are better than me?" Teri felt her hands starting to tremble.

Victoria shrugged her shoulders. She picked up her thousand dollar bag. "Look, none of this matters. Can we just drop it?"

Teri never felt so small before. She wanted to spit out all her details, tell Victoria how she got into all types of prestigious colleges but chose Rhodes because she wanted to stay in Memphis. She wanted to tell her how she could work in any hospital in the country but chose to stay local because she wanted to, but in the end she knew it wasn't going to matter. Nothing she could say would change Victoria's opinion. She was just a dyke from Memphis with a lower pay grade than hers.

"You need to get the fuck out of my house, and never fucking contact me again." Teri looked Victoria directly in her eyes. She wanted to make sure she understood just how serious she was.

"Oh, Teri, don't be like that. In the end all that matters is that we were having fun." Victoria tried to put her arm around Teri who quickly pulled away.

Victoria pulled her keys out of her purse. She looked at Teri glowering back at her.

"Well, I guess it's a good thing I'm going back to Atlanta. See I have a few amazing offers on the table so I'm going to go back home and decide where I want to go. I thought we could have a good-bye fuck but I guess that isn't going to happen."

“Guess not.” Teri held her position.

Teri almost found Victoria’s cockiness amusing. Not only did she come in her house and completely insult her, but she actually thought she was going to get some sex after everything. Teri decided to take the initiative: she walked to the front door and held it open. Victoria held her head high as she walked out. Before Victoria could say anything else Teri slammed the door in her face.

Teri stood in her doorway holding on to the little bit of confidence she had left. Teri couldn’t help but question herself. She wondered what was so wrong with being a pharmacist. She made a lot of money doing what she did and easily could have been a doctor if she wanted to be. Her status had never been questioned before. She didn’t like it.

A guilty feeling overwhelmed her. She thought about all the women she dated who she did the same thing to. Teri fell against her wall; she felt horrible. There she stood pissed at Victoria when she wasn’t any better. There had been millions of times she looked down on women because of their professional status. She was a snob and didn’t even realize it. Out of nowhere, Porsha entered her mind.

Teri grabbed her phone. She scrolled to Porsha’s number. She wanted to call but didn’t know what she would say. Porsha probably hated her. What would she say to a woman she dumped for no good reason? Teri pressed the message button.

> I know you probably hate me but you crossed my mind. I am having a birthday party at Restaurant Bleu on Sunday and would love if you came. Teri

She wondered if she was going to receive a message cursing her out, or a call to tell her just where she could stick her invitation, but she got nothing. Teri knew what that meant. If a woman cursed you out that meant they still had some type of feeling. But when they didn't care to respond at all, it meant they were completely over you. Teri suddenly wanted to call every woman she had ever dated but knew she shouldn't open that can of worms. Karma came back to kick her in her ass, and she knew she was just going to have to take it.

Chapter 27

The next three days were perfect. Willow woke up in the arms of Katrina each day. Katrina spent the mornings with her, showing her more sites of Memphis, and went to the restaurant at night to work the busy dinner rush. The restaurant was booming but Katrina found a way to make it work. They weren't sleeping together; each night Katrina came back tired. They just fell asleep in each other's arms.

"Are you sure about this?" Katrina questioned as she rubbed Willow's head.

The couple sat on a blanket overlooking the pond at Shelby Farms Park. Figuring out they wanted to be together was done; now they had to figure out the rest. The plan was for Willow to move to Memphis.

"I told you, I'm okay with it." Willow smiled.

"I just feel real bad about making you move from your home. I mean you own your place and it's a big-ass deal to come from London to little ol' Memphis."

"I don't care where I stay as long as I am with you."

Katrina leaned in, planting a sweet peck on Willow's lips. It only made sense for Willow to come to Memphis since Katrina was just opening her restaurant. She was going to design her clothes and open a small boutique in Memphis. Things were coming together. Willow was going back to London to get herself together; then she was moving back to America.

"I gotta get home and figure out the visa situation and everything."

"Why not just stay here and never go back? You can live like an illegal alien like a lot of people."

Willow hit her giggling girlfriend. "No, I'm thinking that a visiting visa should suffice. If not I might have to enroll in a university or something."

"Are you nervous at all?" Katrina asked Willow.

"Why would I be nervous?"

"What if you get here and realize you hate my black ass?" Katrina smiled.

Even though joking, the thought entered her head. What if they realized they really didn't want to be together? Katrina would feel horrible for uprooting Willow from her whole life.

"Hey, life is a gamble right? If this doesn't work out I can always find me another woman."

Katrina pinched Willow for her comment. Even with the uncertainties Katrina knew Willow was the one she wanted to be with. Everything else would work itself out.

Katrina thought about Saura; she hadn't talked to her in days. She was afraid to go by her house, fearing what Saura might do or might have done to the house. Teri scolded her, saying she was setting herself up to come home to find herself cleaned out. Katrina didn't worry about it. She was floating on a cloud, and if Saura did wreck anything she would just replace it. It would give her reason to start completely new with Willow.

Katrina dropped Willow back at Devon's house. She headed to the restaurant to prepare for the dinner crowd. She pulled up to the restaurant to see Saura's car parked in her personal parking space. Katrina knew something was up.

"Hey, boss," Misty said as she rolled silverware. "There's a woman waiting on you at the bar."

Katrina looked up to see Saura sitting in a sexy leopard pencil dress nursing a martini.

"All right, thanks." Katrina took a deep breath, bracing herself for the worst.

She walked up behind Saura who was laughing at a joke the bartender told her. She seemed to be in good spirits, which was a plus.

"Saura." Katrina leaned against the bar. "What's going on?"

"Hello, love." Saura flashed her million dollar smile. She looked amazing and she knew it.

"Um, hi, what's up?"

"I just needed to talk you real quick. Don't worry I'm not here to cause a scene."

The two headed to Katrina's office. Saura walked in and took a seat in the chair in front of her desk. Katrina closed the door, hoping no one overheard whatever was about to happen.

"So I've decided to just go ahead and accept the situation. I left you and unfortunately in this case I snoozed and I lost." Saura shrugged her shoulders.

"Saura, I don't want you looking at it like that."

"Well it is what it is. Don't worry, I'll be all right. I think I am going to try my luck in Atlanta, you know they call it the black Hollywood."

Katrina wanted to let out a sigh of relief. Saura seemed to be in a good space and that was all that mattered in the end. "Well if there is anything I can do to help you—"

"Actually there is. I know you mentioned helping me get a place. Well are you willing to help me with that but for Atlanta?"

"Sure, I can help you with moving expenses."

"I'm going to have to stay at our—I mean your—place for a little longer while I get things together. I hope you don't mind."

Katrina shook her head. "Not at all, it's cool."

The two looked at each other for a minute before Saura stood up. Katrina walked her to the door. Katrina tried not to notice how good Saura looked in the dress.

"Oh tell Teri I said happy birthday. What strip club is she making you go to?"

Saura and Katrina laughed.

"Actually we are doing something different. Celebrating right here."

"Oh, that should be nice. Well I have things do to. I'll talk to you later."

Katrina couldn't help but watch Saura as her butt switched out of the kitchen. Katrina noticed all the men in her kitchen staff staring as well. She was excited things were finally coming together. Saura was okay and she had Willow. Things were working out better than she could ever imagine.

Chapter 28

The restaurant was live. Devon was able to book Teri's favorite band to play. They prepared a special VIP area for Teri and their associates and coworkers. Katrina prepared a menu of all of various renditions of Teri's favorite foods, everything from Buffalo chicken skewers to fried macaroni and cheese.

A custom two-tier cake sat as a centerpiece surrounded by fancy pastries and various fruits along with a chocolate fountain. A specialty drink was created in honor of Teri including a mix of vodka and rum.

Teri arrived with two women walking her to her private area as the band played one of her favorite songs. She was already liquored up as she high-fived people who came out to celebrate her birthday.

Willow stood to the side with Ming and Carlos. Carlos looked amazing in a simple suit that fit him perfectly while Ming sported a black suit, white shirt, with a red and white bowtie and ruby red sparking shoes.

"This is amazing," Willow said to Ming who was on his third Teri cocktail.

"Oh, honey, this is normal for these bitches. For Devon's thirtieth birthday she threw herself a party in the zoo and arrived on the back of a camel. It was fabulous."

"Just wait until your birthday. I bet Katrina pulls out all the stops," Carlos added causing Willow to blush.

The three watched as the friends hugged each other. Willow loved the friendship they had. It made her miss her crazy friend Piper.

"Happy birthday, buddy," Katrina said rubbing Teri on the top of her head.

"Thanks thanks, and fuck this party is amazing. I fucking love you guys." Teri's words were already slurring.

"Teri, you might want to take it easy; you have the whole night ahead of you." Devon tried to hand Teri a bottle of water, which she frowned at.

"Just you don't go getting drunk and throwing up again." Teri threw her arm around Devon.

"Or kissing other people's women." Katrina shot an evil glare at Devon who looked off, still slightly embarrassed for kissing Willow.

"Hey the night is early. I might go slip Willow the tongue too." Teri rubbed her hands together.

"Ain't no fun if the homies can't have none!" Devon and Teri high-fived.

Katrina was not amused.

The band took a break and the DJ started spinning. The dance floor filled quickly as Nicki Minaj's latest hit blasted through the restaurant. Willow danced with Katrina, who couldn't keep her hands from under Willow's short melon skater dress. Willow showed off a few London moves when a song she loved came on. Devon tried to pick up the moves but was not a great dancer.

A line dance played. Katrina showed Willow how to do it as the whole crowd moved in unison to the song. The next line dance was so new only a few people knew it, Ming and Carlos being two of the main ones doing every move perfectly.

The DJ started playing old school hip hop. Katrina couldn't believe how hype Willow got when "Push It" by Salt-N-Pepa played. After the old school set the DJ slowed it up a bit, playing a sexy song by Miguel. Willow moved her hips against Katrina. She turned around pressing her butt against Katrina. Willow slow wound her body down and back up Katrina. Katrina bent her over as her butt gyrated to the beat.

Saura stood by the bar, her eyes fixated on the steamy dance in progress on the dance floor. She felt her blood starting to boil. She was supposed to be out on the floor, not some British bitch. She could hear Beyonce's "Ring the Alarm" playing in her head. She had listened to the song a million times in the last few days. She had enough; she wasn't going out like that. She slammed her martini glass on the bar breaking the stem.

Devon sat back in a booth talking to a cute stud she'd seen around a few times before. The girl was not only attractive, but a history professor at the University of Memphis. Her hair was short, as she had just started locking her hair. The woman asked Devon a question, but as she was about to answer she saw Saura slam her glass on the bar.

"Oh shit." Devon jumped up. She looked at the stud who was confused by her actions. "I'm sorry just give me one moment. Don't move, please, don't leave."

Devon proceeded to try to make her way through the crowd.

Teri held a shot in her hand. She stood with Ming and Carlos about to toast to her birthday. Ming's face dropped.

"Teri, um, isn't that sexy blackanese chick Katrina's ex?" Ming pointed causing Carlos and Teri to look at Saura who was rushing toward the unsuspecting couple.

"Oh shit." Teri rushed fighting her way through the crowd.

"Well come on, honey, we might get something for World Star," Ming said following Teri toward the dance floor.

Katrina felt a hard tap on her back. She turned around to see Saura standing there fuming.

"Saura, what are you doing here?"

"So you just gon' embarrass me like this. How dare you bring this bitch around everyone we know!" Saura pushed Willow's shoulder.

Katrina quickly jumped in between them. "You need to go!" Katrina yelled.

"Fuck does she have that I don't have? She's not half the woman I am!"

"Excuse me?" Willow finally had enough of Saura.

Katrina snapped her head around toward Willow.

"Let me handle this," Katrina barked at Willow. "Saura, you got to go." Katrina tried to grab Saura's hand but she jerked away.

"Fuck you, Katrina. You are a fool. Do you know that? What do you fucking know about this girl? Nothing, Absolutely nothing. And you want to leave me for her?" Saura yelled.

The crowd was now watching the spectacle as Saura turned her attention to Willow.

"What do you know about my woman? Do you know any of her family? No, because they all love me! I bet you feel all happy because she's with you. Well she was just between my legs a few days ago and I bet you she will be back!"

Willow was speechless. She turned her head to Katrina who looked at her with guilt written all over her face. Saura continued to bark questions at her.

"You will never be me! You are just something fun for now. A little foreign science project. Katrina is mine. She will be back."

The room was spinning. Willow wanted it all end. Katrina continued trying to contain Saura but she wasn't moving.

"Saura, girl, what are you doing? This is not the time or place for this," Devon said as she tried to grab Saura's arm.

"Let go of me. I thought you two were cool with me and on my side. You got this whore living in your house. Fuck both of you!" Saura pushed Devon.

"Okay where is security before I lose my cool?" Devon motioned for the staff to get security.

"So what you trying to get me, put out? That's great. Have me put out the place I helped you achieve. I found this building. I rooted you on. I supported your dream, and you leave me for this bitch! You know what fuck you and all of this. I don't need this shit!"

Katrina watched as Saura pushed people out of her way. Katrina turned around to Willow who was physically startled.

"Are you okay?" Katrina rubbed Willow's arms.

"I'm fine."

"Fuck you, bitch!"

All of a sudden Saura appeared behind Willow. Instead of leaving she turned and came around the side. She pulled Willow's hair pulling her to the ground. Willow grabbed Saura's dress, pulling her down on the ground with her.

Katrina and Teri tried to break the girls up who were stuck in a hair-tugging battle. Carlos ran over, picking Saura up off the ground. Katrina forced her hands open letting go of Willow's hair. Saura fought to get out of Carlos's strong grip. Security grabbed her, putting her over his shoulder as he carried her out of the restaurant kicking and screaming.

"Baby." Katrina rushed to the aid of Willow. She helped her up.

"Fuck, this is some fucking bullshit!" Willow pushed Katrina away from her.

Willow was pissed. Never did she expect to be in a fight in the middle of a restaurant. She had gone her whole life without ever fighting, and the moment she fell for a woman she got in a brawl.

"I want to go, now!" Willow snapped as she stormed off the dance floor.

"Take her home. I'll take care of things here," Devon said to Katrina who was standing in the middle of the floor with her hands on her forehead in complete disbelief over what just happened.

The couple drove in complete silence all the way back to Devon's house. Willow slammed the car door as she stormed to the back of the house. Katrina sat in the car, not sure how to deal with the situation at hand. Things had gotten out of control. She knew Willow had a reason to be upset.

Katrina gave Willow a few minutes by herself to calm down. She finally opened the door to the guest house to find Willow sitting on the side of the bed still fuming from the events. Katrina sat in the armchair. She didn't know what to say.

"I can't believe this happened," Willow finally spoke.

"I don't know what to say. I am so sorry, Willow."

"Why was she even there?"

"I don't know. No one invited her."

Suddenly it hit Katrina. She had mentioned the party to Saura when she came to her office. She wanted to slap herself for the slip up. She had no idea Saura would show up.

"Was it true?"

"Huh?" Katrina questioned.

Willow looked directly at Katrina. She wanted to see her face when she answered the question. "Was it true? Did you sleep with her?"

Katrina felt the walls closing in on her. She knew she couldn't lie. She lowered her head. That was all Willow needed. She jumped up and grabbed her suitcase. Katrina watched as Willow started throwing her clothes in the bag. Katrina rushed over and grabbed Willow's arm.

"Wait let me explain." Katrina tried to hold Willow who pushed her off.

"There's nothing to say. You weren't supposed to be doing anything with either of us and you slept with her."

"I didn't mean to. I was drunk. That's not an excuse but please wait!" Katrina begged. Katrina grabbed Willow's arm, pulling her close to her. Willow fought to get away but couldn't break free of Katrina's strong hold.

"Let me go!"

"No, Willow, you have to believe me."

"No!" Willow mustered up all her strength to break free. "I trusted you and you lied to me. You let her make a fool of me tonight!"

"I am so sorry. It was a mistake," Katrina begged. "I promise it won't happen again."

"Get out!"

"Willow." Katrina felt like someone hit her with a car.

Katrina stood helpless as she watched the tears rolling down Willow's angry face. She didn't want to leave, but knew staying could only make things worse.

"Willow, I want you. I don't want her. I made a mistake and I regret it so much. But that doesn't change how I feel about you."

"I don't want to talk about this anymore. Please just leave me alone."

The trembling in Willow's voice broke Katrina's heart. Defeated she left the guest house. She stood outside the door as she watched Willow disappear into the bathroom. Katrina didn't know what to do. She wanted to travel back in time and erase everything but she knew she couldn't.

Willow sat on the edge of the bed. She didn't know if she wanted to scream or cry. When things were finally shaping up in one fell swoop everything changed. She wanted to get out of the city. She had gone her whole life without a physical altercation and now she had two within a few days.

Willow all of a sudden felt completely alone. She picked up her tablet, happy to see the green light next to Piper's name was on. She pressed talk and in moments her friend's face appeared on the screen.

"Willz, it's been like forever, chick. What's upper?"

Willow noticed that Piper was wearing one of her outfits. She was too exhausted to question her about it. Willow explained all that happened that night. Piper for once didn't interrupt; she let her friend pour her heart out about the entire situation. They sat for a moment in silence after Willow finished explaining.

"Willz, I really don't know what to say besides it's kind of what you signed up for."

"I didn't sign up to be fighting bitches and shit." Willow rolled her eyes.

"But you said you were willing to go to war for her. Well, you did. At least you don't have any physical battle scars."

Willow fell back on the plush pillows on the large bed. She held the tablet up over her head. "Why does it have to be like that? Why should I have to fight for something I want?"

"Because if it's not worth having if it's not worth fighting for," Piper replied. "I loved Corrie and no matter all our issues I was willing to put up with them because I felt she was worth it."

"Was it really worth it though? Considering all the things and the way it ended?"

Piper thought about the question for a moment. A smile formed on her face. "Yeah, it was." Piper nodded. "We had some fucked-up shit, but we had some amazing shit, too. I like remembering the good stuff. I mean, Will, whatever you decide in the end, you can't say that it hasn't been one amazing ride."

Willow and Piper said their good-byes. Willow turned over, pulling the comforter over her head. She had to admit it was a roller coaster; she just didn't know if she wanted to continue to ride.

Chapter 29

Teri didn't remember how she got home and had no idea who was cooking food in her kitchen. She stumbled out of bed and headed down her hallway. She bit her bottom lip when she saw a chick with an incredible, thick, round ass standing by her table wearing a pair of high-cut panties that didn't hold any of her ass. The woman turned around and smiled.

"Porsha?" Teri rubbed her eyes as she walked into the dining room.

"Hey, I figured you would need some breakfast after last night."

Teri sat down at her bar. Porsha sat a plate with two Belgium waffles in front of her. She poured Teri a glass of orange juice.

"Let me apologize for whatever I might have done last night."

Porsha laughed. "We didn't do anything. I knew you were drunk so I drove you here."

Teri looked up at Porsha. "I don't remember driving to the restaurant."

Porsha shook her head. "You didn't. I drove you here in my new car. I bought me a little used Mazda 6."

"Oh that's cool. Congrats," Teri said chomping down on a bit of one of the waffles.

"Thanks. It's used but it gets me to where I need to be."

"That's all that matters." Teri smiled. There was something different about Porsha, but she couldn't put her finger on it.

Porsha stood up and headed to the kitchen. Teri watched through her bar window as Porsha cleaned up the area she used to make the breakfast.

"Oh and whoever you been fuckin' needs to start grocery shopping. You lucky that box of pancake mix fell out of my grocery bag and I found it in the back of my car."

"What makes you think I've been fucking someone?"

Porsha shrugged her shoulders as she wiped the counter. "Well let's call it wishful thinking. I would hate to believe you just broke it off with me for absolutely no reason at all. The best thing I could think of was something better came along."

Teri felt an ache in the pit of her stomach. She knew she didn't handle things right. "Look about that—"

"You don't have to say anything." Porsha shook her head.

"No, I really want to explain." Teri put her hand on top of Porsha's.

"Okay, well explain. Why did you do it the way you did? I really liked you. I thought you liked me too."

Teri realized how terrible the truth was going to sound. She left Porsha because of her background, when now she found herself being treated the same way by Victoria.

"Honestly, I can't explain. I think I'm not a person who is looking for serious and I saw it coming and needed to end it before things got too heavy. In the back of my mind I thought it would be the better thing."

Porsha pressed her plump lips together as she nodded her head up and down. She stood up. "It's cool. Hey not that I thought it was going to be anything real anyway. I mean I'm not dumb, but I know I wasn't really on your level."

"My level?" Teri gave an inquisitive gaze.

"Come on, you are super educated and stuff. I am just a regular girl. I knew I would never fit in with your group of friends or colleagues."

"Porsha." Teri felt the horrible feeling in her stomach again. She was at a loss for words; she knew everything Porsha was saying was true, even if it was messed up.

A big smile came over Porsha's face. "But you know what? You actually helped me more than you know. When you stopped messing with me I realized just how much of an effect you had on me." Porsha sat back in the chair holding Teri's hand. "I was sitting at home furious listening to my roommates talking shit about you in our small little apartment. I never want to come to your house so bad, not because I wanted you, but just because I missed the space and silence."

Teri and Porsha both laughed.

"Seriously I knew I hated my job and that I could be doing so much more. So I applied at ServiceMaster and got on with Terminix in sales. I'm making an insane amount of money and they have tuition reimbursement so I am now enrolled at Southwest."

"No, shit. You go then, girl." Teri high-fived Porsha.

Porsha was gleaming with pride. Teri realized that she never truly paid attention to more than Porsha's body. Sitting at the table, with no makeup on, she was able to see just how beautiful Porsha really was.

"Speaking of I'm totally going to be late for work so I need to get out of here."

Porsha and Teri stood up. She grabbed her purse and Teri walked her to the door.

"Hey if you ever need anything you have my number. Seriously use it," Teri said as she gave Porsha a hug.

"I will do that, 'cause this math stuff is going to be the death of me." Porsha laughed.

Teri watched until Porsha drove away in her little car, realizing that karma truly was a bitch, but there always was hope for second chances.

Chapter 30

Katrina had so many things she wanted to say but she couldn't figure out the right way to say them. She watched in silence as Willow gave her bags to the ticket agent and got her boarding pass.

Willow woke up the day after the party to find Katrina sleeping in the oversized chair. She wondered how long she had been there. As she watched her she knew that Katrina was still the one she wanted to be with, but she didn't know if she possessed the fight that was needed at that time.

Katrina woke up to see Willow staring at her. She sat up, rubbing her eyes from the terrible sleep. She came back to the guest house that night to plead her case only to find Willow sound asleep. She wanted Willow to be the first thing she saw in the morning.

"How are you feeling?" Katrina's voice cracked.

Willow pulled her knees into her chest. She sat on the bed staring at her gorgeous love. "I'm good."

"Willow, I know last night was bad but I just want to let you know I called Saura and told her to get out of my house. I am done with her and I promise you nothing like that will ever happen again."

Katrina's pleading melted Willow's heart. "I don't think anything else like that would happen, but, I think that I still need to go back to London."

"What?" Katrina stood up. She crawled into the bed, putting her hands on Willow's knees.

Willow put her hands on top of Katrina's. She fought back her emotions. "I think that we both just are moving too fast. I mean Saura might be crazy but she made some valid points. Katrina, we haven't known each other long and I was thinking of moving, changing my whole life to be with you. You didn't have time to get over Saura and we didn't have much time to even truly get to know each other."

Katrina and Willow sat in a silent room. Katrina thought about her words. She knew Willow was right, but she didn't want to let her go. "But, Willow, that's how we get to know each other. Isn't that half of the experience?"

"It is, and I do want to still get to know you, but not living here. I can't just up and move my whole life until I know for sure this is what we need to do."

Katrina felt defeated. If Willow moved back to London she knew it would be the end of them. She didn't want a long-distance relationship. She wanted to be able to feel her mate.

"I don't know if I can do the long-distance thing, Willow." Katrina felt horrible but she had to tell the truth.

Willow hated to hear it but she couldn't be mad. She knew it would be asking a lot and wasn't sure she could handle a long-distance relationship either. But she knew moving to Memphis was a gamble she wasn't ready to make.

Willow thanked the agent and picked up her passport and boarding pass. She walked over to Katrina who was doing everything possible to keep a strong appearance.

"So you got everything you need?" Katrina asked as she handed Willow her carryon backpack.

"Yeah, I do. So I will call you when I land, okay?"

Both women stood in the busy terminal, completely oblivious to anything going on around them. All that mattered in that moment was them.

"Willow, I don't want this to end," Katrina blurted out.

Willow wiped the single tear that fell from Katrina's face. Never in a million years did she think Katrina would start crying before her. She took a deep breath trying to hold in her emotions.

"I don't look at it as ending; it's just a pause." Willow smiled.

Katrina put her arm around Willow, pulling her close to her. She rubbed her hand through Willow's hair for the last time. It was killing her; she didn't want to let go. Willow finally pulled away.

"I gotta go," Willow said as Katrina rubbed her arm.

Willow put the backpack on her back and proceeded to head to her security checkpoint. Tears streamed down her face as she walked away. She knew she couldn't turn around or she might not make it to the gate.

Katrina stood in the terminal surrounded by people, but she never felt more alone in her life.

Chapter 31

Katrina pulled into the restaurant parking lot to see Devon's and Teri's cars parked next to her space. She walked into her office to find them sitting there.

"Hey, friend, drink?" Devon held up a bottle of red wine.

"Sure." Katrina sat in her office chair as Devon poured three glasses of wine.

The friends sat in silence, watching Katrina's face for a sign of what to do or say. They could tell she had been crying from her red, puffy eyes. Katrina downed the glass, holding it out for Devon to refill.

"So she got on a flight?"

"Yeah, they even waived the change fee." Katrina stared at the glass of wine.

"Well damn, it's gotta be the accent. I gotta learn how to talk like I'm British." Teri's attempt to crack a joke fell on deaf ears.

"Katrina, it's not over; you guys can Skype and all that. She even said she will come back." Devon patted her friend on the back. "And we can always go to London. I mean I really don't need an excuse to go to Europe."

"Hey, I will even go," Teri added.

Katrina and Devon both looked at Teri in shock.

"Yeah, I said it. I am trying to turn over a new leaf here, people," Teri huffed.

Devon and Katrina looked at their friend. The three burst out into laughter at Teri's expense. Katrina couldn't stop laughing. Suddenly things didn't seem as bad.

"You know now that I think about it we really were moving pretty fucking fast." Katrina sipped her wine.

"You really were," Devon agreed. "I mean hell it's only been like two months."

"It feels like so much longer." Katrina poured some more wine in her glass.

"That's because you were moving at the speed of dyke," Teri said causing them to laugh. "Seriously you know how we do. You meet, you kiss, and you move in all within the span of seventy-two hours."

"Then you break up three months later and feel like it's the end of the world," Devon added.

"Yeah, until you go to the club and meet the next ex."

All the women laughed. Katrina stood up. She held her glass out toward her friends. "To us. We might be single but we have each other."

The women laughed as they clicked their glasses together.

Six Months Later

Willow and Piper sat on the steps of the Trevi fountain. Willow sipped hot chocolate while she watched Piper flirt with two Australian guys. She never understood why Piper loved to flirt with men, even though she had no intention of ever sleeping with a single one of them.

Willow pulled her new camera out and began to snap photos of the fountain. She noticed a couple kissing on the far side of the steps. She smiled clicking her camera lens to capture the romantic moment.

"You know stalking is against the law."

Willow knew she had to be hearing things. She shook her head as she put the camera back to her eye.

"So you just going to ignore me?"

The voice was oddly familiar. Willow turned around to see Katrina standing behind with a black pea coat and black and silver sweater on.

"Oh my God, what are you doing here?" Willow jumped up off the step.

"Hey, Willow, you couldn't come here during the summer huh?" Teri said as she pulled her scarf up around her ears.

"Can you stop complaining and just take in the moment? We are in Rome!" Devon threw her hand in the air and spun around.

Teri didn't seem as enthused.

"I can't believe you guys are here." Willow walked up the steps to join them.

"Surprise!" Piper joined the group. "We planned this the moment we decided to come."

Piper and Devon's eyes locked on each other. Piper smiled, rolling a piece of her blond hair around her finger. She held her arm out. "Hi, I'm Piper." Piper batted her eyelashes.

"I'm Devon." Devon smiled as she shook Piper's hand. The two immediately walked off from the group.

"Okay, that's some bullshit. I'm cold. I'm going in one of these cafés." Teri walked off.

Katrina hugged Willow. The two didn't realize how well a long-distance relationship could work after all. Due to modern technology it didn't seem like they were apart at all. They talked multiple times a day by Skype. The distance gave them time to actually talk. They learned more about each other than they ever could imagine.

"I can't believe you are here." Willow couldn't stop smiling.

"Well when you told me that you and Piper were going to take a week in Rome I thought that wasn't fair. Rome is our place."

"Oh it is?"

Katrina nodded her head. Willow pressed her lips against Katrina's. No matter how great their video chats were nothing was as good as the real thing. They couple watched as Piper recorded Devon throwing coins into the fountain.

"So should we do that again?" Katrina said as she held on to Willow. "See if it will bring us back to Rome again?"

Willow smiled as she watched the spark growing between Piper and Devon. She stared at the beautiful statues and the cascading water falling down into the giant pool. It was cold, but suddenly she felt warmer than she had felt in a very long time.

Katrina pulled something out of her pocket. She held her hand out reveling four coins. Willow shook her head as she closed Katrina's hand.

"Okay, but only one coin this time. I already have all the love I want."